Cover designed by Maxine Smith

Maxine Smith
Visit my website at www.maxinesmith.co.uk

Printed in Great Britain

First Printing: October 2018

ISBN- 9781726825498

ONE ACT PLAYS

Combination, Rosie the Spoon Polisher, Claude is in the Garden, The Arrival of Dead Dick's Box and A Downmarket Tragedy

Maxine Smith

Also by Maxine Smith

Drama

All Together Now! – A Collection of Monologues

Clearing Up Mrs Treeves and *The Kiteman*: Two Stage Plays

Gutrot and Pigface

Oakes' Last Run

The Order of Ten

The History of Kevin Figgins: A youth play

Vaulting Ambition: A full-length farce for the stage

Prose

The Trials of Kedlewash Village: A Collection of Short Stories

What Happened Karen?

Maxine Smith

Performance Rights

Rights of performance for all or any of the plays in this collection are controlled by the author. The author may issue a performing licence on payment of a fee and subject to a number of conditions. This play is fully protected under the Copyright Laws of the British Commonwealth of Nations, the United States of America and all of the Berne and Universal Copyright Conventions. All rights, including stage, Motion Picture, Radio, Television, Public Reading and translation into foreign Languages are strictly reserved. It is an infringement of the copyright to give any performance or any public reading of this play before the fee has been paid and the licence issued. The Royalty Fee is subject to contract and subject to variation at the sole discretion of the author.

Details of Royalty Fees and how to apply for a performing licence are available upon request. Please use the contact form on the author's website
www.maxinesmith.co.uk
or email directly
maxinesmithplaywright@yahoo.co.uk

About this edition:

Combination, Rosie the Spoon Polisher, Claude is in the Garden, The Arrival of Dead Dick's Box and *A Downmarket Tragedy* were originally published separately and under copyright by New Theatre Publications.

Table of Contents

Combination   6

Rosie the Spoon Polisher   29

Claude is in the Garden   61

The Arrival of Dead Dick's Box   88

A Downmarket Tragedy   121

Combination

She's everything,
even she's when
treated like nothing.
-R. H. Sin

Synopsis

Set in 1961 in the back room of a corner shop, shop workers elegant, sassy Lou and frumpy Elsie are about to enjoy half day closing. Elsie, who lives above the shop, is worried about her missing cat, who she finds ailing in the back yard.

Suddenly two robbers burst in, demand access to the shop's safe and tie the women up. Under pressure the women reveal the location of the safe and Elsie is forced to help Robber 1. Lou is left alone with Robber 2 and it comes to light that Robber 2 is a girl who previously worked at the shop and she is having a baby by Bill Jackson, the man who owns the shop. Furthermore, Robber 1 is her elder brother and the robbery is revenge against Bill Jackson for his abandonment.

Robber 1 returns, angry that the safe has a combination lock and Elsie only knows two of the six numbers needed. Robber 1 then drags Lou off to assist him with opening the safe, as she also knows two numbers. Elsie begs Robber 2 to untie her so she can look after her cat. Once untied, Elsie straggles the cat to put it out of its misery.

Having gained four of the six combination numbers, Robber 2 realises that Bill Jackson had given her two numbers, just like Lou and Elsie hold two numbers each. Robber 1 exits to make a final attempt on the safe, leaving the three women alone to discuss their various relationships with Bill. Lou had an affair with him long ago resulting in an illegitimate daughter. Elsie reveals, much to Lou's shock, that she has more recently been having a relationship with Bill. The women are reflecting that they must have all three been some sort of joke to him, when Robber 1 bursts in explosively, furious that Bill Jackson has left the safe empty. At this point the robbers decide to depart, leaving the shop workers tied up. Robber 1 counsels that they will gain nothing by revealing this incident and even sympathizes with Elsie about her cat. At the last moment, however, he changes his mind and shoots Lou through the head and then turns the gun on cowering Elsie. As the stage descends into darkness, two shots rings out.

Cast

LOU - Manageress of a grocer's shop. Early 30's. Elegant and possibly quite tall (at least she wears high stilettos). Traces of a local accent but she has tried to refine her voice.

ELSIE - Assistant in a grocer's shop. Early 30's. Plump and clumsy in appearance.

ROBBER 1 (TED) - Tough with a volatile temper. Late 30's. Plain, non-descript clothing and a woolly hat pulled down low.

ROBBER 2 (JILL) - Late teens, slight and boyish. Wears a donkey jacket and overalls (or similar) and has a scarf wrapped around her face. She looks convincingly like a boy, although female.

Combination was an Award Winning Finalist in Rotherham Arts One Act Play Competition 2006 and first performed by "On the Road Again Productions" at RCAT Studio Theatre, Rotherham on 8th September 2006. The production was directed by Karen Mulcahey and the cast was as follows:

Lou – Laura Patching
Elsie - Claire Gascoigne
Robber 1 – Gavin Roberts
Robber 2 – Karen Mulcahey

Setting:
Backroom of a Grocer's shop in an industrial town, early spring 1961.
The room is basic and functional, acting as both stockroom and staff rest room. One door adjoins the shop, another to the backyard and a third to the flat where Elsie lives above the shop. Various large boxes of stock stand around in piles. A tall cupboard, its door long ago replaced by a curtain on a wire, stands a alongside a white Belfast sink. Beside the sink is a gas ring. A "clapped out" armchair and a wooden stool stand at the centre of the room, marooned either side of a tatty rug. To complete this dismal picture, a coat stand dominates another corner and on it hangs a green shop coat, a more elegant raincoat and a pale custard-coloured cashmere cardigan.

1pm on a wet Wednesday afternoon. It is half day closing and gloomy. In the shop (off) the door bell jangles as the last customer departs and we hear the bell on the till and the sound of the heavy till drawer being banged shut. A whistling kettle has been left to boil on the gas ring. ELSIE enters, huffing and puffing, coming down from her flat. She is a little perplexed as she searches for her cat. She opens the door to the yard and calls.)

ELSIE: *(With despair)* Fiddle! Fiddle! Fiddledee! Puss, puss, puss!

(Enter LOU from the shop. She immediately sinks into one of the armchairs)

LOU: Thank God for half day closing!

ELSIE: He's not been home all night. I've searched everywhere I can think of.

LOU: Who? Your cat?

ELSIE: Who else? I haven't seen him since yesterday. I'm worried sick. *(Calling out of the door again)* Fiddle! Fiddle!

LOU: Shut the door Els; I'm freezing. Why Scott went to the Antarctic when he could have come to the back room of Jackson's Grocers is beyond me.

ELSIE: He's never been missing like this before.

LOU: He's a cat, not your bloke! Come on, sit down and make the best of it. It's your afternoon off.

(ELSIE shuts the back door and reluctantly sits on the stool, giving a heavy sigh.)

LOU: He'll come back. Cat's, boomerangs and blokes all have that in common.

ELSIE: Huh!

(LOU kicks off her shoes and sighs with relief.)

LOU: Witches at the stake didn't endure this agony to their piggy-wiggies!

ELSIE: Are you surprised? Stuffin' your feet into those things all day.

LOU: What's wrong with them?

ELSIE: Nothing – apart from murdering and torturing your feet and the moaning and groaning that goes with it.

LOU: Els, you're so pragmatic.

ELSIE: Prag what? Look Lou, how's your daughter? How's Angela?

(LOU gives her a stony stare. The kettle boils and the whistle starts to shriek.)

LOU: *(Coldly)* We won't start that again.

ELSIE: *(Pleasant – with a sarcastic edge)* Cup of tea?

LOU: Please.

ELSIE: Perhaps we should have a cake as well.

LOU: I'll see what's left.

(LOU stands just inside the shop and calls through.)

LOU: Jam doughnuts, jam tarts, cream puffs – they all ooze red stuff.

ELSIE: I'll have one of all of 'em.

LOU: Els!

ELSIE: Oh, go on. Remind me I'm as fat as that Michelin man.

LOU: You're not fat.

ELSIE: Go on.

LOU: A bit comfortable and rounded, but not fat.

ELSIE: Don't try and cheer me up now you've upset me.

LOU: It wasn't what I meant.

ELSIE: Oh no!

LOU: I just wanted you to see that if we demolish every cakes left on the counter, Jacko will notice and start on again about us chomping our way through the stock. He sees us as piranha's swarming around his profit margin like it smelled of human flesh. You know Jacko and his profit margin.

ELSIE: I'll give you that Lou. You're *so* creative when you've put your very elegant foot in it.

LOU: You're missing the point.

ELSIE: Look, them cakes will be stale as corpses by tomorrow and we'll have to chuck 'em out. There'll be nothing for his profit margin but the stink of decaying pastry and rancid cream.

LOU: Jacko won't look at it that way, will he? Be sensible Els. You don't just work here – you live over the shop. You lose your job, you lose the roof over your head. He can be very vindictive.

ELSIE: Well you're the manageress and if you want to threaten me with the almighty boot...

LOU: ...for Goodness sake Els!

ELSIE: Never mind. Does your daughter wear shoes like that?

LOU: (*Bitterly*) Look, have as many cakes as you want. Indulge yourself. I'll pour the tea then I'll help you look for your blessed cat.

ELSIE: I don't think I want a cake now. I've gone off the idea.

LOU: The mice have been in the sugar again.

ELSIE: How do you know that?

LOU: They've left the evidence - footprints.

ELSIE: Jacko says you get sniffy about that sort of thing.

LOU: Nonsense! That's why he let you keep your cat when you moved in upstairs. Thought it would keep the rats down. Ironic really, since he's such a rat. Anyway, fine job Fiddle's doing. Mice in the sugar, rats in the coal house and a rat for a boss. Perhaps I should put rat poison down. *(Beat)* Not for the rats though.

ELSIE: Jacko?

LOU: Last time we had mice, before you came, he left the poison next to an open jar of sherbet. I always said he was dangerous around two things – food and women – and look, here he is, with a grocer's shop and a tarty little wife! Bill Jackson, Family Grocer, part time poisoner and full time deliberate b......

ELSIE:...Why do you hate him so much?

LOU: I don't – well, I suppose I do. It's not important. Have you looked in the outside lavatory?

ELSIE: I've been all over. Wish I knew where he was.

LOU: Come on Els. Just have one cake. You'll be doing the customers a favour. If Jacko lets them stay on the stand just one more day they'll grow legs and do their own death march to the cemetery. As you said, nothing left but rot and decay.

ELSIE: You've changed your tune. *(Calling:)* Fiddle! *(To Lou:)* I'll have a doughnut *(Calling:)* Puss, puss, puss!

(LOU goes through to the shop. We immediately hear someone banging loudly on the front door of the shop)

LOU: *(Off)* We're closed.

(The knocking continues)

LOU: *(calling off)* The sign says "closed".

(LOU returns with a donut in a paper bag.)

LOU: There's your cake.

(The knocking starts again.)

LOU: For goodness sake!

ELSIE: Who's knocking?

LOU: The blind's down and I haven't developed x-ray vision yet.

(The knocking continues.)

LOU: I suppose I'll have to unlock and tell them to push off. Have you looked in the back alley?

(LOU goes back through to the shop and ELSIE goes out to the yard. A little while passes before ELSIE returns holding Fiddle in her arms. The cat is in a poor state, limp and possibly mewling pathetically. She takes an empty cardboard box and places it on the floor. She lines it with a towel from beside the sink. Carefully, she nests Fiddle in the box. She crouches beside the box, very concerned, gently stroking the cat. A moment later LOU appears in the door way and stands very still.)

LOU: *(Softly)* Els.

ELSIE: He's not well, poor little thing. I don't what's happened. He's been lying out there for hours, in some weeds by the fence. I never noticed him. I never heard anything. I feel terrible. He must think that I can't be bothered.

LOU: *(Softly)* Els.

ROBBER 1: *(Voice off)* Get in there.

(LOU is pushed forward and for the first time we see that ROBBER 1 has been standing behind her with gun pointing in her back. ROBBER 2 quickly slips into the room and points a gun at ELSIE. ELSIE gasps and puts her hands up in submission as though she was in a cowboy film. She looks from Robber 1 to Robber 2 and then points at the cardboard box while keeping one hand still in the air.)

ELSIE: He's still breathing. You can see he's breathing, can't you?

LOU: Yes, he's breathing.

ROBBER 1: What's she talking about?

LOU: It's her cat. She couldn't find him and now she has.

ELSIE: What's happening Lou?

ROBBER 1: Just shut it, the pair of you!

LOU: *(With some spirit)* Just what the heck do you want?

ROBBER 1: *(Roaring)* Shut up!

ELSIE: Please, please don't hurt my cat.

LOU: *(Firmly)* You shouldn't be in here. It's half day closing and we were about to have our afternoon off.

(ROBBER 1 now thrust his rifle in LOU's face)

ROBBER 1: Shut up, you stupid woman.

(LOU nods her head and because the rifle is lodges against it, the rifle moves up and down, looking rather ridiculous.)

ROBBER 1: Now slowly and without opening your mouth again I want you to shut the back door and bolt it. Are you clear about that?

LOU: Okay.

(LOU extracts herself from the butt of the rifle and closes the back door.)

ROBBER 1: Now you sit there, on the stool and the fat one can sit in the chair.
(ELSE and LOU sit as instructed. ROBBER 2 starts to quickly bind their wrists with rope from her pocket. ELSIE submits easily and with fear but LOU is more deliberately awkward).

ROBBER 1: For the purpose of this situation, you call me Ted and he *(gesturing to ROBBER 2)* is Jack.

LOU: I didn't think we'd be socializing. How well-mannered of you - would you like me to make afternoon tea?

ROBBER 1: Shut up woman. Are you stupid? This is a siege – act scared, like I'm about to blow you head off.

LOU: And are you?

ROBBER 1: *(Coldly:)* The temptation is almost overwhelming.

ELSIE: *(Hissing:)* Shut up Lou!

ROBBER 1: That's right. Your fat friend catches on quickly.

LOU: *(Very quietly:)* Full marks to Elsie.

ROBBER 1: Did you say something?

(LOU shakes her head)

ROBBER 1: Hopefully we won't need to talk much or be here long and then, ladies, you can enjoy the rest of your afternoon.

LOU: Don't worry yourself about that. My bus left five minutes ago.

ROBBER 1: Did I make a mistake in thinking you wanted to carry on drawing breath?

LOU: Just my way of getting along – funerals, air raids, sieges, that sort of thing.

ROBBER 1: You'll get along if you listen. It's easy. We know there's a safe and we know that one of you must know how to get in it. We know it's half-day closing and there'll be no members of the public to disturb us – no "have-a-go-Joes" to foul it up. If you co-operate it won't take long. Do you both understand? Can I say it more plainly? *(To ELSIE)* You?

ELSIE: We understand.

ROBBER 1: *(To LOU)* And you, Mouth Almighty?

LOU: I think we've grasped the thread.

ROBBER 1: Good! I'm glad of it.

LOU: But...

ROBBER 1:...She's off again! Do you know what's good for you?

LOU: But you're assuming that our understanding will also lead to our co-operation and it doesn't.

ELSIE: Don't speak for me Lou. Just do what he wants and let's get this over.

LOU: We're not co-operating.

ROBBER 1: You're bloody bonkers! I'm pointing a gun at your bloody head and I'll blow it off. You're in a bloody siege.

ELSIE: Oh no, stop it. He's having a fit.

ROBBER 1: You're right, I'm having a fit.

(ELSIE throws herself on her knees beside the cardboard box. ROBBER 2 lurches forward and holds the gun close to her, jerking "his" head to look at Robber 1 in panic.)

LOU: She didn't mean you. It's her cat. He's not well.

ROBBER 1: One flaming mad woman's enough to deal with. Why didn't we do the Co-op instead?

ELSIE: Please untie me! I have to look after him.

LOU: For God's sake untie her. She's too fat to run off.

ROBBER 1: *(Roaring)* Shut it!

LOU: What is it Els? What's the matter?

ELSIE: Fiddle! Poor Fiddle. He keeps twitching. I'm begging you. Please untie me.

LOU: Untie her. She's got to look after the cat. See, he's being sick. Are you going to make him lie in it?

(ROBBER 1 pulls the yellow cashmere cardigan from the coat stand.)

ROBBER 1: *(To Robber 2)* Here, mop it up.

LOU: *(affronted)* That's my cardi; it's cashmere.

ELSIE: Hush Lad. Hush Fiddle. I don't know what's wrong with you. I don't know how to help.

LOU: *(Quickly)* We'll do a deal with you. That cat needs a vet. Let her call the vet.

ROBBER 1: Deal with it when we've gone. God, that cat stinks. Look, this has gone far enough –it's a bloody pantomine. I know how to put an end to this. *(Forcefully, to Robber 2)* Shoot the bloody thing.

(ELSIE screams and ROBBER 2 backs off shaking "his" head.)

ROBBER 1: Go on, shoot it! All right, I'll do it and we'll get on with what we came here to do.

(ROBBER 1 points the gun into the box and then drops it again a moment later.)

ROBBER 1: This beggars belief! It's peeing itself, filthy sod. Didn't you house train him?

ELSIE: He can't help it. He's poorly – we've tried to tell you.

ROBBER 1: It wants shooting. *(ROBBER 1 raises his gun again but this time LOU leaps in front of the butt.)*

LOU: Stop!

ROBBER 1: A bloody hero. We really need a hero now.

LOU: Don't shoot the cat and we'll tell where the safe is.

ROBBER 1: We'll have no bother finding it.

LOU: Yes, you will. It isn't easy to find.

ROBBER 1: All right, but let's get on with it. Jesus, I feel like I'm in a three act farce! *(To ELSIE)* You, fatso, come with me.

LOU: She's not in charge. I am. I'll take you to the safe. Els doesn't know.

ROBBER 1: The faster you learn who's really in charge the better for all of us. She's coming with me, like I said. I don't want you rattling on in the background. *(To ELSIE)* Do you know where the safe is?

ELSIE: Underneath the sacks of rice and flour.

LOU: How did you....?

ELSIE: ...You'll need a screwdriver to take up some boards. Bill had it sunk into the floor below the floorboards.

ROBBER 1: And the screwdriver?

LOU: Didn't you think to bring one?

ELSIE: There's a tray with odds and ends underneath the counter where the till is. The screwdriver's in there.

ROBBER 1: We're going to get this done fast now.

LOU: Is it worth all this trouble? For one day's takings?

ROBBER 1: What now?

LOU: Well, there's money in the till from this morning of course, but it isn't much. Things are always slow on Wednesdays. Bill Jackson came and collected the last week's takings yesterday afternoon to bank it.

ROBBER 1: Bill Jackson's got you fooled Mouth Almighty. Do you really think we've only come for a day's takings? Do you really think you know what's in that safe now? There's stuff in that safe that Bill Jackson wouldn't want to put in any bank.

ROBBER 1: *(To ROBBER 2)* If she starts, shut her up. Do whatever you have to. *(To ELSIE)* Which way?

ELSIE: We haven't got a key.

ROBBER 1: *(Drawing a large key from his pocket)* Well I bloody well have.

(ELSIE shoots a desperate, appealing look at LOU)

LOU: Just show him where the safe is. I'll watch the cat.

ELSIE: Back through the shop.

ROBBER 1: Move yourself.

(ELSIE exits through to the shop followed by ROBBER 1. ROBBER 2 sits in the chair and with perceivable nervousness points the gun at LOU. There is silence for a little while)

LOU: You're talkative. You've done nothing but chat, chat, chat. *(Looks down at the box)* Poor animal. Doesn't look good. Oh! He's being sick again – blood this time, both ends and he's twitching. This is really bad. You'd better get Els back here. Go on!

(ROBBER 2 goes to the entrance to the shop. "He" calls though while keeping the gun trained on Lou)

ROBBER 2: Oi!

(After a few moments ROBBER 1 returns dragging ELSIE by the arm)

ROBBER 1: What's going on?

ROBBER 2: Cat. *(Jerks head toward the box. ELSIE gives a cry of despair)*

LOU: It needs a vet.

ROBBER 1: They can get a vet after we've gone. Go on you. *(Shoves ELSIE back into the shop)*

LOU: You've let it lie there in its own sick. Are you just going to stand there and watch it bleed to death as well? Untie my hands for a minute so I can see to it.

ROBBER 2: No.

LOU: You can hold the gun to my head the whole time. I won't do anything apart from cleaning up the cat. Els has pampered that cat all of its life until it's not got any dignity anyway. We don't have to let it die in that mess.

ROBBER 2: Be quick.

(ROBBER 2 unties LOU'S hands and she gets down and tends to the cat.)

LOU: You're very familiar. Did you know that? You used to work here didn't you? You're not even a bloke. Your name's Jill and you used to work here until Bill Jackson sacked you.

ROBBER 2: Jesus Christ.

LOU: Do you think that scarf around your face really hides who you really are? I can still see your eyes and the way you walk and stand, even the way you hold that gun. You're a woman – well a girl anyway.

ROBBER 2: You're wrong.

LOU: I remember you swatting flies in that shop, just out there, on a summer's day – not last summer, the one before. Different weapon but the same person in control though. Same Jacko as well; too mean to let us use a fly paper out of the stock.

ROBBER 2: Ted's right. You just don't know when to shut up.

LOU: Are you going to shoot me now because I can tell the police exactly where to look?

ROBBER 2: Leave it Lou.

LOU: See, you remember my name well enough to be free with it. This is no game for a girl. You've got yourself into a right mess. I know that working here wasn't exactly thrilling, but you're going to end up in clink. Why are you wound up in something as barmy as this? Who's the other one? Is he your boyfriend?

ROBBER 2: What's it to you?

LOU: I think he's a bit old for you actually. About twice your age.

ROBBER 2: He's my brother. *(Harshly)* Hands!

(LOU puts her hands out so that ROBBER 2 can bind her wrists again)

LOU: What's he doing leading you into this? You're just a kid.

ROBBER 2: I'm nineteen. You were younger than that!

LOU: Younger than what? What are you talking about?

ROBBER 2: You and Bill Jackson. You had a baby.

LOU: *(Beat)* Angela.

ROBBER 2: And he didn't marry you.

LOU: How do you know all of this? Why do you know all of this?

ROBBER 2: Bill told me.

LOU: And when did you see Bill last? When did he tell you? I would have thought you'd be the last person. He called you a useless lump before he gave you the boot.

ROBBER 2: He pays Angela's school fees. She's out of the way at a boarding school.

LOU: That's private and not open for conversation. Not with you anyway. But tell me, what is this? Revenging yourself on Bill for giving you the boot.

ROBBER 2: Christ, he's given me more than that!

LOU: What does that mean?

ROBBER 2: It doesn't mean anything.

LOU: There's more to this....look, when did you last see Bill Jackson?

ROBBER 2: Not long enough ago.

LOU: What did he do to you? Don't look so surprised, I know what he is, sniffing around any woman he can. But it isn't worth ending up in jail on account of that dirty old bugger.

ROBBER 2: He's got to pay.

LOU: I suppose he will when you brother's yanked the front off that safe.

ROBBER 2: We need that money and there's a lot of it; he's up to all sorts. If anyone should be in jail, it's him.

LOU: Is it worth all of this?

ROBBER 2: I've got to have that money.

LOU: Are you having a baby? Bill Jackson's baby? Is that what this is all about?

(ROBBER 2 starts to cry.)

LOU: Good Lord. There's more scruples in a pile of monkey droppings than in Bill Jackson.

ROBBER 2: Our Ted went mad when he found out about it. I thought he'd kill Bill but then he said he's find another way to make him suffer.

LOU: It's a comic book revenge. I can't believe anyone is this stupid.

ROBBER 2: *(Sudden anger)* I don't know why I'll telling you this lot? You were a cow to me when I worked here.

LOU: You were a lazy madam. *(Shrugging)* What do you expect?

(ROBBER 1 returns pushing Elsie in front of him. ROBBER 2 hastily pulls the scarf back around her mouth.)

ROBBER 1: There's a soddin' combination on the safe and she only knows two numbers. *(To LOU)* I know you know what it is, so out with it. Now!

LOU: I don't know any numbers.

ROBBER 1: Of course you bloody do! I've had enough of this.

(*ROBBER 1 gives ELSIE a vicious shove with the butt of his rifle sending her reeling on to the floor*)

LOU: Stop that! Leave her alone and I'll tell you. It's forty-seven. Bill told me to remember that number. I don't know why. Forty-seven.

(*ROBBER 1 drags LOU roughly by the arm.*)

ROBBER 1: You come with me! If you're making this up, I'll knock your block off!

(*Exit ROBBER 1 and LOU. ROBBER 2 points the gun at ELSIE. ELSIE half gets up and scrabbles over to the box to look at the cat. She looks for some moments in silence.*)

ELSIE: Please help me. Please. I just want to hold him, to comfort him. Just untie my hands. I promise I won't do anything but pick up the cat. Please.

(*ROBBER 2 ignores ELSIE. ELSIE crawls over to ROBBER 2'S feet and speaks even more imploringly*)

ELSIE: Please, help me. I just want to hold my cat. Untie my hands. I won't try to get away. Honestly, I won't.

(*Impulsively, ROBBER 2 unties ELSIE'S hands. ELSIE goes to the box. She reaches in and strangles the cat. ROBBER 2 stands transfixed.*)

ELSIE: There. A job done properly.

(*ELSIE slumps back exhausted and puts her hands to her face.*)

ROBBER 2: Why did you do that?

ELSIE: It was the last bloody merciful thing I could do.

ROBBER 2: I feel sick. (*She rushes over to the sink and throws up.*)

ELSIE: You'd better have a glass of water.

ROBBER 2: Get in that chair don't move.

(ROBBER 2 thrusts her gun at ELSIE)

ELSIE: You sound like a ....

ROBBER 2: A girl! Yes, I sound like a girl.

ELSIE: Why are you doing this?

ROBBER 2: You think I'd tell you.

(ELSIE shrugs. There is the sound of a commotion. ROBBER 1 returns dragging LOU cruelly by the hair.)

ROBBER 1: I said this was a bloody farce.

ROBBER 2: What's happened?

ROBBER 1: Either they're lying about the numbers – and I'll have to blow their bloody faces off – or it's a six digit safe!

LOU: You're a bastard!

ROBBER 1: Shut your cake hole before I fill it with led. You *(to ROBBER 2)* keep the pair of them covered while I work this out. *(After a few moments)* Somebody knows those bleeding numbers and they'd better say so.

LOU: We've done all we can.

ROBBER 2: Ninety-four. A number I was told never to forget. He told me.

ROBBER 1: I hope you're bloody right. Just kept these two here while I finish off.

(The three sit in silence for a few moments)

LOU: The cat?

ELSIE: I know. I dealt with it's misery.

LOU: Oh Els.

ROBBER 2: Sick bugger.

(LOU shakes her head.)

ELSIE: Bill gave me that cat before I came to work here. I used to baby sit his kids and I had a budgie then. It died and I was really upset about it so Bill bought me the cat.

LOU: Not like him to be so kind.

ELS: He's always been kind to me.

LOU: Well I don't think that is the universally held experience of Bill Jackson, Els.

ELSIE: I was wondering; isn't it strange that we should all know some of the numbers? Thirty-two, forty-seven, ninety-four – a bit of the combination for each of us. We **are** the combination and we're not much else and the three of us don't have much in common apart from that.

LOU: Apart from Bill. Not something to boast about. *(A thought strikes her.)* Hey Els, why should Bill tell you two of the numbers?

ELSIE: Why shouldn't he?

LOU: There's more to this Els. Was there something going on between you two?

ELSIE: What do you mean? I hope you're not suggest...

LOU: That's exactly what I'm suggesting. The numbers and the way you always went on about my Angela, badgering away. You were jealous, jealous of me and Bill. Christ almighty!

ELSIE: You always thought I was too fat and clumsy for anyone to give me a second look. Why shouldn't I have a man?

LOU: Well you've picked a good one. A man who pushes out fatherless children like he flogs sacks of potatoes.

ELSIE: It's possible to be more careful than you were Lou.

LOU: I was a kid. I didn't know my backside from my larynx. But, you know, I don't think you're bothered about Bill and I really. You're jealous of Angela, of me having a kid when all he gave you was a cat.

ELSIE: That's cruel.

LOU: I wasn't trying to be but if you're jealous over Angela you're going to be green all over in a minute! *(pointing to ROBBER 2)* You see her...

ROBBER 2: ...Hey, shut it!

LOU: No, you shut it. *(Turning again to ELSIE)* Well, she's got a bun in the oven and guess who's the father?

ELSIE: Her boyfriend out there obviously.

ROBBER 2: Boyfriend!

ELSIE: How should I be expected to know?

LOU: It's Bill you idiot. He takes just about every woman he meets for a ride – even at his age. Oil and charm still gets him a long way and why we all fall for, it I'll never know.

ELSIE: Two numbers each. We're a sad crowd. None of us really **have** him or **had** him.

LOU: This is Bill Jack we're discussing Els, not Frank Sinatra.

ELSIE: It's like some joke he's playing and we're the butt of it. *(Signs)* Three butts to keep him laughing.

LOU: Laughing! Her brother'll be laughing when he sees inside the safe.

(ROBBER 1 enters, angrier than ever)

ROBBER 1: Bastard!!! He's cleaned it out.

ROBBER 2: What?

ROBBER 1: There's nothing in the safe.

ROBBER 2: You mean we've wasted our time.

ROBBER 1: *(trying to regain some control)* Have you talked to them?

(ROBBER 2 shakes "his" head)

ROBBER 1: Sure?

LOU: She hasn't said a word to us, have you?

(ROBBER 2 shakes her head again.)

ROBBER 1: *(To ROBBER 2)* Quick, get out of here...

ROBBER 2: ...but...

ROBBER 1: ...wait for me in the back alley. Go on.

(Exit ROBBER 2)

ROBBER 1: Right, we're going to leave you now ladies. You know it will be a good idea to say nothing to anyone. You won't gain by it. *(To ELSIE)* Look you, I'm sorry about the cat.

ELSIE: Thank you.

Robber 1: *(To LOU)* I'll untie these before I go.

(ROBBER 1 unbinds ELSIE's wrists. She stays seated. He then unbinds LOU'S wrists. She cringes away from him as he does this, for the first time showing her nerves. ROBBER 1 then goes to the door but pauses, turns back and walks up to LOU and holds the gun directly at her head.)

ROBBER 1: You've got a big gob on you.

(ROBBER 1 pulls the trigger and shoots LOU. ELSIE, whimpering and terrified, tries to hide herself inadequately behind the side of her chair. ROBBER 1 watches her, raises his finger to his lips to "shush" her and then raises the gun. Lights fade to black. Two gun shots ring out.)

Curtain

Rosie the Spoon Polisher

I tell you, in this world
being a little crazy
helps to keep you sane.
-Zsa Zsa Gabor

Synopsis

Old Rosie lives contentedly in a post-apocalyptic world, where society is divided into hostile tribes. She likes, as she says, to have fun and order the world to her own "way of dancing". One day she discovers Boz, a young man who has been beaten and left under a bush near her fence. She tends his wounds none too gently and derives much amusement from tricking him into clucking like a chicken and other such games. Boz spins a tale that he got his injuries in a beating sustained for romancing a girl from another tribe on the opposite side of the river.

Things turn sour between Boz and Rosie when he realises the bush by her fence is Cattlebob, an illegal and deadly substance which he assumes she has been processing for her own benefit. He uses his supposed knowledge to threaten Rosie as he wants a share and demands off-cuts from the bush.

This unpleasant interaction is cut short by the arrival of Alf, the piemaker, and Rosie hides Boz in her wood shed. Alf has an interesting story to tell. He is looking for a young man whom he battered the previous evening for breaking into the pie shop, stealing the takings and beating his young assistant, Oswald. Alf has promised Oswald that he will find the "varmint" and let Oswald beat him too in recompense. Realising that Boz is the thief, she doesn't reveal this to Alf but tells him to return with Oswald in one hour. Alf departs and Rosie calls Boz from the shed, where he has heard nothing. She tells him that she will consider complying with his demands and he is pleased at the prospect of starting his own profitable Cattlebob farm. Rosie sympathises with Boz, saying he must be tired and hungry and so she gets him to rest. She then sings him to sleep with a strange song that reflects her own warped perspective on the world; she knows full-well that Alf will return with Oswald to give Boz a second beating.

The play is humorous and exists in another world, having its roots in the absurdist tradition.

Cast

ROSIE – An old woman
BOZ – A young man
ALF – the man who makes pies

Rosie the Spoon Polisher was an Award Winning Finalist in Rotherham Arts One Act Play Competition 2010 and was first performed by "Third Nail Theatre Company" at The Arts Centre Studio Theatre, Rotherham on July 18th 2010. The script was also shortlisted for the Diane Raffle One Act Play Competition in 2010.

(A garden that butts onto a river bank. The area is covered in grass and bushes but for staging purposes, this need not be literal. Centre stage is a dilapidated wooden stool and an old wooden box large enough for an adult to sit on. ROSIE, an old woman, sits on the stool. At her feet is a basket full of spoons of all sizes. She polishes the spoons with a rag. After a while she stops and looks at herself in the bowl of one of the larger spoons. Her expression shows she doesn't like what she sees.)

ROSIE: You remind me of a brown paper bag that's been screwed up in a ball and flattened out again. I could blame the spoon, but the spoon don't lie. Yes Girl, you're a raddled and lined, wind-scorched and scoured old woman. Still, you're happy enough parked here by the river, having your fun and ordering everything to your way of dancing. You make the most of it while you can.

(ROSIE continues to polish the spoons but then she is disturbed by a low groaning sound, off. She looks sharply S.L. and narrows her eyes and sets her jaw. She gets up and exits S.L.)

ROSIE: *(off)* Get up you lazy lummox.

(Groaning off continues)

ROSIE: *(off)* I can see you're not dead.

(Groaning continues)

ROSIE: I'm not standing for this. I've got more than enough to do. You come with me.

(Sounds of a commotion. Louder, more painful groaning that is almost a wailing. Within moments enter ROSIE, bodily dragging BOZ, a beaten young man, on stage. His face, in particular, is battered with cuts and bruises. She pulls him to his feet.)

ROSIE: On your feet you lazy bag of swedes.

(BOZ immediately collapses.)

BOZ: I can't move.

ROSIE: You just did.

BOZ: It's too painful!

ROSIE: Painful? Dipped your hand in acid today?

BOZ: No.

ROSIE: Given birth recently, have you?

BOZ: No.

ROSIE: Had your leg amputated this week without even a swig of rum?

BOZ: No.

ROSIE: Well stop complaining.

BOZ: You what?

ROSIE: You heard me.

BOZ: You should have left me where I lay.

ROSIE: This is my land.

BOZ: I was under the bush *outside* your fence.

ROSIE: The gooseberry bush.

BOZ: I don't know what sort of a bush it was.

ROSIE: Gooseberry.

BOZ: Gooseberry, if you say...

ROSIE: ... I do. I know exactly what it is. It's mine and the roots are on my land.

BOZ: You should have just left me there.

ROSIE: For what?

BOZ: I'd have moved on eventually, when I got myself together or someone found me.

ROSIE: You were found.

BOZ: Not by you. I didn't ask you to find me. I wanted someone I know; one of my own tribe.

ROSIE: Your tribe? Who are they?

BOZ: They'll come looking for me.

ROSIE: Do you know what tribe I'm with?

BOZ: No. You could be from either side of the river.

ROSIE: Yes, I could. Enemy or friend; you just don't know.

BOZ: You should say which you are. Here or there? Us or them?

ROSIE: Tough. I'm telling you nothing.

BOZ: Can't I just get back under the bush?

ROSIE: No.

BOZ: But why not? I don't see the problem.

ROSIE: I couldn't stand the chow-row.

BOZ: You what?

ROSIE: The groaning. The racket you were making. It disturbed my work.

BOZ: What work is that?

ROSIE: I polish spoons.

BOZ: You make a living from that?

ROSIE: None of your business.

BOZ: Do you always lead folk to questions and then cut them off?

ROSIE: How did you get in that state?

BOZ: *(smugly)* None of your business.

ROSIE: I see. Tit for tat is it? I won't give you my financial details and you won't tell me how you got the sage and onion kicked out of you.

BOZ: You what?

ROSIE: Stuffing.

BOZ: I'm not a dead chicken.

ROSIE: Do you cluck?

BOZ: Of course I don't cluck.

ROSIE: So, that's your proof.

BOZ: Proof? Proof of what?

ROSIE: That you're a dead chicken.

BOZ: You what?

ROSIE: I repeat, that you're a dead chicken. If you're a live one, you'd cluck.

BOZ: I'm not. I just told you I'm not.

ROSIE: Not what?

BOZ: Er...er...a dead chicken.

ROSIE: So you're a live chicken?

BOZ: Ey?

ROSIE: So you'd better cluck.

BOZ: No.

ROSIE: Go on cluck.

BOZ: No.

ROSIE: Cluck.

BOZ: No way.

ROSIE: Prove you're alive.

BOZ: This is daft.

ROSIE: Cluck.

BOZ: No, no, no.

ROSIE: Cluck, cluck, little chick.

BOZ: I'm not little and I can't cluck.

ROSIE: You can. Any live chicken can cluck.

(*BOZ pauses for a moment, looks at Rosie and then makes a few weak chicken clucking noises.*)

ROSIE: Louder. I'm old. I'm deaf.

(*BOZ clucks more loudly and boldly.*)

BOZ: Satisfied?

ROSIE: Yes, I'm satisfied, but are you?

BOZ: Yes.

ROSIE: Mmmm.

BOZ: What's "mmmm" meant to say?

ROSIE: It's always been my understanding that roosters crow, not cluck. So that makes you a girl, not a lad, even in the chicken world?

BOZ: I'm not playing this game anymore.

ROSIE: Not just one quick cock-a-doodle-do?

BOZ: This is ridiculous.

(*ROSIE laughs wildly*)

ROSIE: I've always enjoyed winding up the male of the species.

BOZ: Shut up old woman. I've had enough and I'm in pain.

ROSIE: Please yourself.

(*ROSIE goes back to polishing her spoons. BOZ raises himself and sits on the box and starts to inspect his injures, stiffly and painfully.*)

ROSIE: Let's have a look at your injuries then.

BOZ: I don't know you.

ROSIE: That's probably a good thing since you were just sitting in my garden making fowl noises for all you are worth. Now, let's see.

(ROSIE grasps BOZ's head roughly to inspect his injuries.)

BOZ: *(in pain)* Owwwww! Steady on.

ROSIE: Hurt does it?

BOZ: What do you think?

ROSIE: Nasty.

BOZ: I'll say you're nasty. Spiteful! Wicked!

ROSIE: What happened to you?

BOZ: I can't say.

ROSIE: You were there when it happened, unless it was an out of body experience.

BOZ: I mean I'm not telling you. I don't have to. I don't choose to.

ROSIE: Please yourself, but you were found under my bush. That gives me certain rights.

BOZ: Rubbish. Bilge water.

ROSIE: What do you want most in the world at this moment?

BOZ: To not hurt.

ROSIE: Those cuts need some iodine.

BOZ: You can leave me alone.

ROSIE: I will, but only for a jiffy.

(*ROSIE exits. BOZ goes to the basket of spoons. He looks at several and then polishes one on his sleeve. Obviously, this is painful. He then holds it up and looks at his face in the bowl of the spoon and doesn't like what he can see. He then looks around cautiously before slipping the spoon into his pocket. Re-enter ROSIE with a bottle of iodine and another rag, just in time to see the theft; ROSIE is annoyed.*)

ROSIE: Move away from the spoons.

BOZ: What?

ROSIE: Hand it over. Come on, the one you nicked.

(*BOZ takes the spoon from his pocket, feigning nonchalance.*)

BOZ: It's just a spoon.

ROSIE: Put it down.

BOZ: Okay.

ROSIE: You've not got permission to touch the spoons. I'll say when there can be spoon-touching and it's not yet.

(*BOZ tosses the spoon back in the basket.*)

ROSIE: And what about the polishing rag? Have you been pawing that about as well?

BOZ: It's there in the basket.

(*She pokes in the basket and is satisfied that all is in order.*)

ROSIE: I'll say when you can touch the spoons. Now let's have a look at you.

BOZ: I don't want looking at, not by you, you old crow.

ROSIE: This won't hurt.

(She douses the rag in her hand with iodine.)

BOZ: I haven't given my permission yet.

ROSIE: And I'm overriding your objections. Permission is just a fallacy for the gullible who believe in it.

BOZ: But you just....

ROSIE: More fool you. Now hold still.

(ROSIE holds the rag firmly to one of the cuts on BOZ's face. BOZ yelps loudly in pain.)

ROSIE: That doesn't hurt does it?

BOZ: I'm only crying because it's so pleasurable.

(ROSIE removes the rag and screws the top back on the bottle of iodine.)

ROSIE: That should do. It won't fester now.

BOZ: Aren't you going see to the other cuts?

ROSIE: No, I've done the biggest one.

BOZ: What's the point in just dousing the one? I'm tough enough to take it. I've done iodine before.

ROSIE: The cut I just treated; well, you won't have anything to compare it with if they all heal, will you? Then, you won't know how lucky you are.

BOZ: Give me the iodine. I'll do it myself

ROSIE: No, I'm in charge of the iodine. Now tell me, what's happened to you?

BOZ: I'm saying nothing.

ROSIE: You just did.

BOZ: I mean, I'm not saying anything else.

ROSIE: A fight was it?

BOZ: More like an ambush.

ROSIE: So, you didn't participate willingly?

BOZ: I fought back. I'm not chicken.

ROSIE: Yet you cluck, cluck, and cluck.

BOZ: You tricked me into that.

ROSIE: Merely encouraged. Now let's have a look at that arm.

(ROSIE grabs BOZ's arm and pumps it up and down. BOZ yelps in pain.)

ROSIE: It still works but it might be a bit sore.

BOZ: It's agony.

ROSIE: Did they kick you there?

BOZ: They jumped up and down on it.

ROSIE: It's not broken. How many were there?

BOZ: Three or four. Maybe five or six.

ROSIE: You were lucky. They could have torn you to pieces and eaten up the bits.

BOZ: I feel like I've been torn to pieces.

ROSIE: Here, take a spoon.

(ROSIE proffers a spoon from the basket to BOZ)

BOZ: You what?

ROSIE: Take one.

(BOZ, bemused chooses a spoon from the basket)

ROSIE: Look into the bowl.

BOZ: What am I looking for? The future?

ROSIE: No, you own stupidity.

BOZ: Where do I find that?

ROSIE: You can see it now.

BOZ: Are you trying to trick me? Not five minutes ago, I wasn't allowed to touch the spoons.

ROSIE: I want you to see. Now, look into the spoon.

(BOZ takes a spoon and looks into it.)

BOZ: My nose is huge.

ROSIE: That's the convex. Turn it over.

BOZ: What's the point of this?

ROSIE: What can you see?

BOZ: Me.

ROSIE: And how do you look?

BOZ: Like me. A few cuts. All my teeth are there. What do you expect?

ROSIE: And how many parts are you made of?

BOZ: Just the one.

ROSIE: So you're in one piece.

BOZ: I didn't need to look into a spoon to find that out.

ROSIE: But how do you feel?

BOZ: Sort of in one piece.

ROSIE: You say you feel like one thing, but you look at yourself and you feel like something like else. You're weak, Chicken, and easily led.

BOZ: *(offended)* Says who?

ROSIE: See, if the bowl of the spoon was shattered, you could see dozens of you; one in every fragment. What would you do then?

BOZ: I don't know.

ROSIE: You'd say "I feel like I'm in a thousand pieces!"

BOZ: I wouldn't!

ROSIE: You'd throw your arms around yourself and try to pull all the bits back together again.

BOZ: No.

ROSIE: You'd probably even try to secure it all together with bit of rope.

BOZ: I didn't mean it literally in the first place. I was just a bit all over the place.

ROSIE: Was the fight literal or was it just a figure of speech?

BOZ: The fight was real.

ROSIE: Now you're talking. You've admitted there was a fight.

BOZ: Okay, I was in a fight, but what's it got to do with you?

ROSIE: It began God-knows where but it ceased under my gooseberry bush.

BOZ: So?

ROSIE: The fruit will be traumatised and there's still a fair amount of the red stuff soaking into my soil. Your blood, my garden. I've got a vested interest and I only want to know the details Chicken.

BOZ: Will you let go of the clucking, old woman?

ROSIE: You volunteered the noises.

BOZ: I did not!

ROSIE: Now, did you start it?

BOZ: You know you started it. Clucking, chickens and cock-a-doodle-do; I been a regular fool to your ways.

ROSIE: I meant, did you start the fight?

BOZ: I was chased.

ROSIE: Serves you right for being on the wrong side of the river. Run you back over my bridge, did they?

BOZ: How do you know what's the wrong side of the river for me?

ROSIE: You smell of this side. So, what happened?

BOZ: It wasn't down to me.

ROSIE: You've come off worse, that much is clear but I how can I really judge the whole thing if you won't tell me.

BOZ: I'm not in a court of law.

ROSIE: No, but I think you need an ally.

BOZ: No more tricks?

ROSIE: You just tell your story young man.

BOZ: Well my tribe is this side of the river. We try to avoid trouble and not go over there very much but sometimes there's temptation for them as well as us. There was a party over here. Some of their lot came over but they weren't causing no bother so we looked the other way. There was this girl that came with them, called Annabel and she were glorious; all high spirits and towering heels, like sniffing a bottle of thinners when you were a kid, and a good dancer to boot. She saw me looking at her and she smiled and twisted her fingers in her hair. Later she met me in the garden and without saying anything she just kissed me. Snogged the face off me, just like that. I like a forward girl even if she's one of their tribe, not ours. But whatever tribe, nothing bothers Annabel; Annabel's got guts. So after that, I would go to her side of the river and we'd meet up. It was secret, it was all right but then they must have found out 'cause when I went to meet up last night she wasn't waiting for me.

ROSIE: She dumped you.

BOZ: No! She just wasn't there but some from her tribe were. They chased me, caught me, beat me and then they dragged me back and dumped me on your bridge.

ROSIE: Are you sure this girl told no one?

BOZ: Of course not. Annabel wouldn't let that happen to me. They must have followed us and watched us one night.

ROSIE: You can think that but in my experience it's usually someone telling someone, and then they tell someone else and then everyone knows.

BOZ: No, we didn't say a word, either one of us.

ROSIE: Are you sure your tribe wasn't involved.

BOZ: Of course not.

ROSIE: But tribes get very odd when one of their own casts their eyes elsewhere. Beatings for the men and tar and feathering for the girls. Of course, if they're already committed to someone in their own tribe, then it's rough music in the middle of the night and they're driven away.

BOZ: You make it sound so glib like it was the way of nature.

ROSIE: It is. Nature's way to sustain hostility. Where would we be without hostility? See this spoon here, you can look into it, it's a bit of shock to see yourself for the first time. If you move your eyes into the middle, you look like you've got big bulbous fish eyes. *(ROSIE looks at her own reflection in a spoon and then sniggers).*

BOZ: I'm not sure you're not doolally.

ROSIE: Fair comment but was I the one clucking?

BOZ: I was caught in your madness. *(Sniffs the air)* What's the smell?

ROSIE: Which one?

BOZ: *(sniffs)* That one.

ROSIE: There's hundreds of smells hanging in the air out here. Let's see *(sniffs theatrically)* Borage, purple lavender, grass, the odd whiff of butterfly pooh and the delicate aroma of the nylon factory and then, there's that most unique of compounds.

BOZ: What's that?

ROSIE: The drains from the old cottages just up there. They've been seeping into the river for donkey's years. Some days I could tell you at teatime what they had for dinner. I'm not too keen on cabbage and bean days myself.

BOZ: We always thought the river was pure, like blue diamonds.

ROSIE: Just like a turquoise sea?

BOZ: Yes, a turquoise sea, lapping on some far-off shore.

ROSIE: With palm trees wafting in a gentle breeze.

BOZ: Yes palm trees, and the coconuts falling into your lap.

ROSIE: And the foaming indigo waves slapping their tongues far enough up the beach to break on your feet.

BOZ: Yes, it feels cool and gentle after a long walk along the sand.

ROSIE: Hot sand skimming the soles of your unshod feet

BOZ: Licked away in the delicate kisses of the blue water tickling your toes.

ROSIE: Could almost be there.

BOZ: You don't need a spoon to see this.

ROSIE: I wouldn't go that far.

BOZ: The blue water and the gentle breeze.

ROSIE: Just like sitting by my river. The blue water.

BOZ: Yes, it's a bit of a miracle, that blue water.

ROSIE: Do you know how it came to be here?

BOZ: You what?

ROSIE: Once upon a time the river wasn't always such a startling colour. Then some clever Dick invented the Looblu and in the housing estate up there it goes into their cisterns by the truckload and when they flush, gallons of it spills into the river. Just like everything else; straight in the river.

BOZ: That's disgusting. You're disgusting. You shatter every illusion.

ROSIE: Oh, I don't know. The Looblue's quite a useful addition; makes it safer to wash in.

BOZ: You wash your clothes in there?

ROSIE: No certainly not, just my hands and face.

BOZ: Knowing what's in there?

ROSIE: I like to keep clean but I don't go for the full immersion. Clean hands is essential in my work; no mucky paws on the clean spoons.

BOZ: And that smell?

ROSIE: It's not me.

BOZ: No another smell.

ROSIE: I've told you, there are thousands of stinks all churned in there together. The air is as packed as a Christmas cake.

BOZ: But there's one distinct smell rises above the rest.

ROSIE: You're using your imagination again.

BOZ: It's real.

ROSIE: It's in your head. In your mind's eye.

BOZ: It's a smell. It's up my nose.

ROSIE: Think about it. It's snot.

BOZ: I can almost touch it.

ROSIE: Just like a bogie. You haven't unearthed a new discovery.

BOZ: It pokes its head up, that smell. Odd – a bit acid, like it would burn your tongue but milky as well.

ROSIE: Leave it.

BOZ: You know what it is.

ROSIE: Leave it.

BOZ: Wait.

(Exit BOZ S.L.)

ROSIE: *(calling to S.L.)* Leave my gooseberries. They're not yours to touch.

(Re-enter BOZ with a handful of leaves and a few green berries.)

ROSIE: You've pulled pieces off my bush.

BOZ: But it's not gooseberry, is it?

ROSIE: Of course it's gooseberry. Taste the fruit if you must. Go on, eat it, seeing as you've ripped it so rudely from its mother ship.

BOZ: Not on your life. All the time I was lying there, underneath it, I knew there was something. Something I've not smelled for a long, long time.

ROSIE: Speculation.

BOZ: Speculation isn't a smell and the smell's not gooseberry either. It's Cattlebob isn't it?

ROSIE: I deny all claims.

BOZ: A banned substance.

ROSIE: What makes you think an old woman like me would be doing growing something illegal Chicken?

BOZ: It's bare-faced cheek, growing it right here on your pathway with people passing up and down every day. So obvious, you'd barely notice.

ROSIE: You've gone completely up a one-way alley.

BOZ: The question is, why grow it? Who do you sell it to?

ROSIE: It's gooseberry, I'll telling you, for jam and pies. Only a complete half wit would mix up gooseberry and Cattlebob.

BOZ: Wrong! That's why it took the authorities so long to eradicate it. It's almost identical apart from the slow painful death that doesn't usually come with your gooseberry tart and cream.

ROSIE: The food of myth and fear.

BOZ: So you admit, it's Cattlebob.

ROSIE: I admit nothing.

BOZ: Well you eat one.

ROSIE: No.

BOZ: Why not? You were keen for me to try.

ROSIE: Gooseberries don't agree with me. They give me indigestion. *(Rosie gives a loud burp).*

BOZ: The easiest way's to cut it open and look at the pips.

ROSIE: Please yourself.

(BOZ dramatically bites a berry in half. ROSIE gestures to stop him but he spits out the half in his mouth anyway. He looks closely at the other half of the berry and gives a loud sneering laugh. ROSIE continues to polish her spoons.)

ROSIE: What's funny Chicken?

BOZ: See the purple pips. Bright, luminous jewels. Purple proof positive that these are Cattlebob.

ROSIE: You shouldn't have poked your nose in.

BOZ: Who'd have thought? Let's see, do they go in a still or have you got some pet alchemist to process them for you for a share in the profits?

ROSIE: I don't get you.

BOZ: Well listen more carefully old woman.

(She puts her hands over her ears. BOZ goes to her and pulls her hands away from her ears.)

BOZ: Boot's on the other foot now. If I go to the authorities with this, they'll find the worst stinking prison cell they've got, fling you in and forget that you ever existed.

ROSIE: I'd have that bush taken down before the story had a chance to leave your mouth.

BOZ: What? Dig it up and burn it?

ROSIE: Probably.

BOZ: The smell would linger in the air for days.

ROSIE: I'd deny it.

BOZ: But there'd be a witness. Me!

ROSIE: You could just let it pass. It's doing no harm.

BOZ: You are funny. It's the most harmful natural substance known to man. I've heard stories. Distil it, add it to food and drink, you don't know it's there. The coroner won't have a clue what happened and can only resort to "died of natural causes". Pour it into the other tribe's water supply and you'll never need to go to war again. So, you see, you've had all the power up till now and this is me getting the upper hand. Go on, tell me, what do you do with the Cattlebob when you harvest it?

ROSIE: Nothing. I just really like the bush.

BOZ: It's an ugly bush and that is a particularly dreadful specimen. You'll have to try harder than that.

ROSIE: It has uses you don't understand.

BOZ: Enlighten me.

ROSIE: I make it into a pulp. It's good for cleaning the spoons.

BOZ: A likely story.

ROSIE: It lifts the tarnish before I polish them.

BOZ: Like nothing else can.

ROSIE: It's a very ancient remedy.

BOZ: I don't buy this old witch stuff.

ROSIE: There's somebody coming.

BOZ: Bilge water! It's too early.

ROSIE: They're coming along the path.

BOZ: I can't see them.

ROSIE: They're not in view yet.

BOZ: So how do you know they're there?

ROSIE: They're definitely coming closer.

BOZ: Who are they?

ROSIE: I don' know.

BOZ: What do they look like?

ROSIE: I can't see them.

BOZ: So how do you know they're coming?

ROSIE: I can feel them. Keep watching.

BOZ: A likely story! Second sight!

ROSIE: No, vibrations through the soles of the feet.

BOZ: *(pointing into the distance)* What's that?

ROSIE: It's them.

BOZ: But who is it?

ROSIE: Keep looking. They're too far off to tell.

BOZ: I can't let them see me.

ROSIE: Why not?

BOZ: They're getting closer.

ROSIE: Do you know them?

BOZ: I don't know. I need to hide.

ROSIE: But the boot's on the other foot.

BOZ: Forget that. Help me.

ROSIE: But the boot's on the path and it's getting closer.

BOZ: I'm going into your cottage until they've passed?

ROSIE: It's locked.

BOZ: Give me the key.

ROSIE: Why should I help you?

BOZ: I don't know; because I need your help.

ROSIE: My shed. You can go into my shed. Just lift the latch. Quick now.

(Exit BOZ. ROSIE sits down to spoon polishing once more. After a few moments enter ALF. He wears a hat and carries a stick, rather more like a baseball bat than a walking stick. He stops when he sees ROSIE and removes his hat.)

ALF: Good morning to you.

ROSIE: You're addressing me?

ALF: Yes, good morning.

ROSIE: I wasn't expecting a visitor this early.

ALF: You're Rosie, Rosie the spoon polisher.

ROSIE: I might be if the right person is asking. How do you know my name?

ALF: I ask, people tell. You all come my way sooner or later.

ROSIE: And what way might that be? You're not....?

ALF: What?

ROSIE: You've not come to collect me because I'm not ready to leave yet. These spoons still need to be polished and there'll be another lot tomorrow and then more and more and more. I don't think I'll be ready for many years yet.

ALF: Just who do you think I am? I don't come to collect anything. They all come to me.

ROSIE: I don't know who you are. You haven't said.

ALF: Alf Bott.

ROSIE: Means nothing.

ALF: Alf Bott Pies.

ROSIE: No.

ALF: I'm the pie maker. Big bakery and shop up in the town. Everyone comes there.

ROSIE: Not me. I like to make my own pies.

ALF: No matter. I'm looking for a dog.

ROSIE: I've seen no dog, not this morning.

ALF: Have you been out here since you were risen?

ROSIE: That's my business. What breed is the dog?

ALF: It's a human dog.

ROSIE: Do you keep it on a chain and collar?

ALF: No, it's not mine but if I had my way....

ROSIE: ...I don't want to hear about your strange up- town and over-the-river habits. I can tell you, I've seen no one, man, dog, cat, rabbit or mouse but it's early on yet. Though there was a chicken at one point.

ALF: He would have been this way in the night. It's more his leaving than his arriving you would have seen.

ROSIE: Who?

ALF: Him.

ROSIE: Doesn't he have a name?

ALF: No doubt, but I don't know it.

ROSIE: So you've lost a man in the dark who you think is a dog and you'd like to put a collar on him but you don't know his name. Good luck.

(*ROSIE goes back to polishing her spoons.*)

ALF: I've not finished with you yet.

ROSIE: Who said you could start?

ALF: Very prickly.

ROSIE: As a porcupine or a yard bush.

ALF: Then you don't have a reputation for mollycoddling.

ROSIE: Then all's well in the world.

(ROSIE picks up her basket and goes to exit.)

ALF: Are you sure there's been no one this way?

ROSIE: Who is this man?

ALF: An uncommon thief.

ROSIE: Has he stolen from you?

ALF: I'll say so.

ROSIE: Why uncommon?

ALF: He's the only one who has ever tried to steal from me.

ROSIE: Tell us the story.

ALF: Why do you need to know? You've seen no-one and I must get on with looking.

ROSIE: He might come this way yet and if I choose to stay in my garden today by way of helping you, then I'm bound to see him.

ALF: True.

ROSIE: I might be more apt to notice him if I know what to pick out.

ALF: I suppose that's a fair point.

ROSIE: So, tell me the story.

ALF: If I can sit down, I'll tell it.

ROSIE: You can have the box. The stool is mine.

ALF: Appreciated.

(They sit.)

ALF: You know I make pies?

ROSIE: Ay, but where does the man come in?

ALF: The varmint!

ROSIE: I think you're not too keen on this man?

ALF: He waited until just after dusk when we were shutting up. My apprentice, Oswald was all alone in the shop. He does my clearing up every day; it's part of his training. Oswald had almost finished and there was a knock on the door. If I've told that lad once, I've told him a thousand times, "Don't open the door to no one once we've shut up". But Oswald thought it was a late customer and being a helpful kind, he went to answer it anyway. The times I've said, "Remember to keep the catch on that door". But anyway, before he could get to the catch, the door burst open.

ROSIE: So, was it the young man?

ALF: It was. He'd used his shoulder and the door just exploded open showering wooden splinters all over the place from the frame where the lock was broken. I dare say he hurt himself in doing it. Oswald said it was like a cannonball coming through and it hit him in the chest and knocked all the wind out. He couldn't get his breath but the varmint still demanded answers to his questions about the day's takings. When Oswald couldn't speak he kept kicking him where he lay on the floor. Then he set to pulling the place apart until he found the money.

ROSIE: Where were you?

ALF: I'd just stepped out to do a thing or two but I got back in time to see the shop door stood wide open, Oswald still lying on the floor and that varmint running away.

ROSIE: What did he look like? Did you see him? Did Oswald see him?

ALF: We both did. I thought he was very young but Oswald said he was older.

ROSIE: It was a dark night.

ALF: Oswald said he had fair hair but I thought he was darker. Oswald said he was less than average height but I took him to be tall. Oswald said he was skinny but he looked to me like he'd been stuffing a fair few of my pies under his belt.

ROSIE: What are you going to do when you find him?

ALF: I chased after him last night and I caught up. It was somewhere out this way. I gave him a good paling with my stick. You can see there's blood on it still.

(ALF shows ROSIE the stick.)

ROSIE: So, he's had his come-uppence. Why do you still need to find him? Did you not get your money back?

ALF: I got that back last night but I told him while he was lying there, that I'd come back.

ROSIE: What for?

ALF: For Oswald. Oswald hasn't had his chance to pail him yet. When I find him I'll drag him back and the lad can have his fair go.

ROSIE: And does Oswald want this?

ALF: I have told him he must do it. He must wreak his revenge and put the world back in balance. And what's more, I'll stand and watch him and make sure he does it well.

ROSIE: So let me see, you're looking for a tall, short, fat, thin man, with dark hair or fair hair, who you left beaten on the highway last night and told him to lie still and you'd be back in the morning so you could watch someone else give him another good beating.

ALF: Ay, that's right. Now I've told you it all, can you help me?

ROSIE: Perhaps if you came back this way in hour I might have something to give you.

ALF: Shall I bring Oswald?

ROSIE: I think you might. May as well be fully prepared because who knows who might come this way and when they do, I'll keep them talking until you arrive.

ALF: Will you do that?

ROSIE: I just told you I would. Now on your way, fetch Oswald and we'll all meet here in an hour.

ALF: Put it there old woman.

(*ALF extends his hand and shakes ROSIE's hand vigorously. He replaces his hat, tips it to ROSIE and then departs. ROSIE sit,s picks up a spoon and starts to polish it again. She pauses, clearly thinking, looks in the direction of the shed and turns to look in the direction that ALF has departed. She replaces the spoon in this basket with an air of certainty.*)

ROSIE: (*calling off*) You can come out.

(*Re-enter BOZ tentatively*)

BOZ: Have they gone?

ROSIE: Nobody here. How much of that did you see?

BOZ: Nothing. There's no window in your shed or even a crack to look through.

ROSIE: But you heard?

BOZ: I heard nothing. Who was it?

ROSIE: Just a neighbour.

BOZ: Someone you can trust?

ROSIE: Can I trust you?

BOZ: For a share in the Cattlebob.

ROSIE: Done.

BOZ: That easily?

ROSIE: I know when to compromise.

BOZ: Will you give me an off-cut to start my own farm?

ROSIE: You can have as much of the bush as you like but before we get down to business you need to sit still.

BOZ: You what?

ROSIE: You had a nasty beating and you've had a busy time of it this morning.

BOZ: I do feel a bit giddy.

ROSIE: Just you sit there. I just need to see to my spoons and then I'll be getting breakfast in a little while.

BOZ: Yes, my stomach's gurgling.

ROSIE: Just think of Annabel.

BOZ: You what?

ROSIE: Annabel. Think of Annabel and it'll take your mind off your gurgling stomach.

BOZ: Oh, ay.

ROSIE: Just let me polish the spoons. You'll feel much better an hour from now.

BOZ: When I've eaten and had a rest.

ROSIE: Yes, in an hour.

(*Rosie polishes spoons and sings. The tune and the voice are soulful and soothing. During the song BOZ becomes drowsy and starts to sleep.*)

ROSIE:

Sun is rising in the west,
Polishing spoons is what I do best,
Carrots for breakfast,
Much better than sex,
Don't forget to wear a vest.

Moon is purple, moon is grey,
Smiling down in the noon of day,
Tar is for drinking,
And river's stinking,
Bury the hatchet in the hay.

Sun is setting in the East,
Polishing spoons is what I like least,
Life is for hating,
Crocodiles mating,
Move the boots onto both right feet.

(BOZ snores gently.)

ROSIE: Sleeping? You snore on for an hour, just an hour and let old Rosie watch you. Let old Rosie watch the world go this way, that way and her way while she polishes the spoons.

(ROSIE starts to hum the tune to the song she was singing. Lights fade down.)

THE END.

Claude is in the Garden

*A man should always consider
how much he has
more than he wants.*
-Joseph Addison

Synopsis

A play for two actresses in a simple domestic setting.

Claude Monet was the most famous of the Impressionist artists working in 19th century France. Rumour suggests that Monet and Alice Hoschede, who he eventually married, carried on an affair prior to the death of his first wife, Camille. The play is based on the broad facts of the situation but the thoughts, feeling and comments of the characters are created by the writer for the purpose of the drama.

The play commences with the voices of Monet and Alice in old age. Alice for the first time tells him of a conversation that took place with Camille in the last months of her life. We go back to a time when Alice was caring for Camille. Camille reveals to Alice the unknown details and hardships of her marriage including Claude Monet's once attempted suicide. The atmosphere is tense because both women are aware of the rumours and yet, quite mischievously, Camille seems to hint at and edge towards an open discussion of the supposed adultery. Alice is nervous and edgy throughout but equally kind and encouraging towards Camille, trying to get her to believe she isn't dying. Camille, takes a hard, more realistic and indeed, humorous view. Nonetheless, she is deeply wounded at the thought of how she will fade from her children's lives. At one point she openly accuses Alice of sleeping with her husband but immediately laughs it off. Behind their conversation is threaded the sense of the artist working away in the garden, entirely oblivious to the two women and their difficult discussion.

As the play draws to a close we return again to the voices of Alice and Claude and his recognition of an unacknowledged cruelty in Camille's treatment of Alice. He soothes Alice so she can sleep and he can return to the garden.

This play offers of opportunity for the actresses to create tense humour in what is a very awkward situation.

Cast

Camille – first wife of Impressionist artist Claude Monet, aged 32

Alice – wife of bankrupt Paris department store magnate, Ernest Hoschede, aged 35

and the voices of:

Claude Monet – in old age

Alice Monet – Monet's second wife, in old age

(It is advisable to pre-record the voices of CLAUDE MONET and ALICE MONET.)

Relevant Background Information:

(Producers of play may find it helpful to include the following information in the production programme.)

Claude Monet was the most famous of the Impressionist artists working in 19th century France. Rumour and debate amongst biographers suggests that Claude Monet and Alice Hoschede may have carried on an affair prior to the death of his first wife, Camille, in 1879. It has also been claimed that Claude was the father of Alice's youngest son, although the child was registered to her husband, Ernest Hoschede. Following Camille's death, Alice and her children continued to live with Monet's family in spite of increasingly prolonged absences on the part of Ernest. After Ernest died, Claude and Alice married and remained together until Alice herself died in 1911. The affair has never been substaniated.

"Claude is in the Garden" is based on the broad facts of the situation but the thoughts, feelings and comments of the characters are created by the writer for the purpose of the drama.

(Blackout. We hear the voices of CLAUDE and ALICE MONET, as the light very slowly fades up to reveal CAMILLE'S bedroom on May 15th 1874, the necessary items being a large comfortable chair and a footstool before it. CAMILLE stands USC wearing a dramatic, red Japanese kimono and a blonde wig. She holds a large white fan. Once fully revealed, she remains static during the conversation between CLAUDE and ALICE MONET)

CLAUDE MONET: (*off*) Alice! Alice! Are you sleeping Alice?

ALICE MONET: (*off*) Come on in. I don't lock the door.

CLAUDE MONET: (*off*) Have I woken you?

ALICE MONET: (*off*) I won't sleep my last days away Claude.

CLAUDE MONET: (*off*) Last days! Utter nonsense!

ALICE MONET: (*off*) No, I'm just staggering towards the exit door this time.

CLAUDE MONET: (*off*) You'll feel better when you've had some proper rest.

ALICE MONET: (*off*) I've been thinking about Camille.

CLAUDE MONET: (*off*) Camille? God rest her.

ALICE MONET: (*off*) She's kept me awake for hours.

CLAUDE MONET: (*off*) But why are you letting that bother you now, after all these years?

ALICE MONET: (*off*) She tormented me, Claude, in those last months.

CLAUDE MONET: (*off*) You've never said anything before.

ALICE MONET: (*off*) And criticise a woman who's dying?

CLAUDE MONET: (*off*) It wasn't your fault.

ALICE MONET: (*off*) I seemed to torture her.

CLAUDE MONET: (*off*) Shush! Why don't you try to sleep now. I'll pull the blinds down.

ALICE MONET: (*off*) And I suppose you'll be in the garden.

CLAUDE MONET: (*off*) Not far away Alice.

(The stage is now fully lit. It is mid morning and sunny outside. CAMILLE walks slowly upstage with some difficulty as she lives with considerable pain. CAMILLE slumps against the back of the chair, overcome by the effort. Knocking at the door, first of all gently and then more insistent. ALICE calls to CAMILLE, her voice soft and concerned.)

ALICE: *(off)* Camille, Camille, are you still sleeping?

CAMILLE: *(quietly)* Not really.

(Knocking continues)

ALICE: *(off)* Camille, Camille.

CAMILLE: Alice.

ALICE: *(off)* Can I come in Camille?

CAMILLE: Of course. I haven't locked the door.

(Enter ALICE. She is a little startled at CAMILLE'S appearance)

ALICE: Camille!

CAMILLE: Good morning Alice.

ALICE: Are you all right Camille?

CAMILLE: You can see I'm up and today I've dressed myself.

ALICE: But what for?

CAMILLE: A joke.

ALICE: You look ready for a party. At least the clothes do.

CAMILLE: A costume party? That's a thought when you're feeling fit to fall over.

ALICE: Can I help you with anything?

CAMILLE: Take the wig off me please. It's as hot as Sicily and tight as a pig's anus.

ALICE: Of course.

(*ALICE gently removes the wig. Beneath CAMILLE's dark hair falls loose and untidy*)

ALICE: Is that better?

CAMILLE: Yes, much cooler. This kimono-thing can come off me as well.

(*CAMILLE starts to pull off the kimono with difficultly but ALICE immediately removes it for her. Beneath she wears a cotton nightgown. ALICE guides CAMILLE to sit in the chair and places her feet up on the footstool.*)

ALICE: How do you feel today? You look exhausted already.

CAMILLE: It's only like someone's trying to pull my guts out with a meat hook.

ALICE: That bad? I'm sorry.

CAMILLE: Don't worry about it. Yesterday I thought someone was trying to cut me in half with a rusty saw.

ALICE: I've been using tincture of rhubarb and henbane for period pains. It's the latest thing.

CAMILLE: You sound like a quack doctor advertising in "La Presse".

ALICE: Do I?

CAMILLE: Yes, you do. "Laxora, the best remedy for constipation, flatulence and general derangement of the organs of the stomach". Anyway Alice, when do you ever have period pains? You're nearly always pregnant.

ALICE: I suppose that's the way it looks.

CAMILLE: I'm sorry Alice, but suggesting rhubarb's a bit like offering a sprinkling of eau de lavender to someone whose leg's just been torn off in a carriage accident.

ALICE: I apologise; it was a thoughtless idea.

CAMILLE: I'm being cruel Alice. Getting dressed up like that took a lot of effort. That was the really stupid idea.

ALICE: What's it about, these strange clothes?

CAMILLE: "La Japonaise".

ALICE: What's that?

CAMILLE: You've seen the painting, haven't you?

ALICE: I don't think I have. Is it one of Claude's?

CAMILLE: I'm disappointed Alice. I thought you'd seen them all. I thought you were Claude's greatest supporter.

ALICE: I don't remember the picture.

CAMILLE: Don't look so worried. It was a few years ago; just Claude's fierce, red conclusion when Paris went mad for anything Japanese.

ALICE: I recall the fashion very well.

CAMILLE: But now we don't live in Paris.

ALICE: Ernest opened a Japanese Department in one of his stores and then he had a whole room at home kitted out with imports. I didn't really like it, but as usual, it was just of Ernest's fads.

CAMILLE: That was Claude's point. He was transfixed if it was just one vase but apparently you needed to stick at least twenty-seven vases on a single mantle shelf! All hideous and overdone, like eating too many pink macaroons; but the vases were even more likely to make you puke.

ALICE: I can't disagree with you.

CAMILLE: Well Alice, it's Claude's verdict you're agreeing with and not me.

ALICE: I tried to reason with Ernest at the time but he would waste money.

CAMILLE: All the fans were falling down in the background, like October leaves that are surprised to be dead.

ALICE: What?

CAMILLE: The falling leaves; all false and theatrical. I was the figure in that painting Alice and now I'm falling down as well.

ALICE: The pain's very bad today, isn't it? Very, very bad.

CAMILLE: Perhaps, but choosing whether to call it "excruciating" or "agonizing" is as hard as deciding whether to have Belgian lace or just a swig of gin. It keeps me busy for hours. Which one would you go for Alice?

ALICE: We should keep some morphine in for days like this.

CAMILLE: I think morphine and I will become excellent buddies far too quickly and then what happens when Claude's got no money and we can't afford it? Where am I then Alice?

ALICE: Claude should find a way to afford it. He'll have to make sacrifices.

CAMILLE: So, you would expect him to go without his colours and canvases?

ALICE: Of course he should.

CAMILLE: Anyone would think you're the artist's wife and I was married to the entrepreneur. Simple business structures – stock, process, sell – do keep up Alice. If he hasn't got the paint, then he can't produce, and there's nothing to sell. No, it's not your problem. I'm saving myself up for the morphine, eventually, and then nothing else will matter.

ALICE: Camille, listen to me. You could get better. By summer next year you'll be out in the garden with Claude and the children again.

CAMILLE: I'm not one of your children Alice. Tell it to the fairies.

ALICE: We all want you to get better.

CAMILLE: I like the collective sense you bring to that; we'll just keep hoping, all of us. Anyway, I wanted to talk to you in private, with no Claude around.

ALICE: When's Claude ever around when the sun's up?

CAMILLE: If you were his wife you'd soon get fed up.

ALICE: I think you're very patient Camille.

CAMILLE: Where is Claude?

ALICE: In the garden.

CAMILLE: Working?

ALICE: With the children. When I came up he was running 'round after them, playing games.

CAMILLE: *(pointedly)* How unusual; running 'round after *our* children.

ALICE: What do you want to talk to me about?

CAMILLE: Did you know that my Claude was writing to your Ernest last night?

ALICE: That's a bit ridiculous. Ernest should be back from Paris by this evening. Claude can talk to him directly.

CAMILLE: He had something important to reveal to Ernest.

ALICE: Did he?

CAMILLE: Yes, he did.

ALICE: Do you know what this thing is?

CAMILLE: I do. Claude read the letter to me.

ALICE: It sounds like something's upset you Camille.

CAMILLE: It did and I know you'll understand why.

ALICE: *(nervous)* Oh.

CAMILLE: Claude put it to Ernest that there was a good reason for our two families to cease living together in future.

ALICE: *(nervous)* Did he give the reason?

CAMILLE: Yes, he did. It's blindingly obvious and you know already, don't you Alice?

ALICE: I'm so sorry.

CAMILLE: He said we couldn't carry on being a burden to you, what with no money coming in and me sick all the time.

ALICE: *(relieved)* Is that all?

CAMILLE: Yes.

ALICE: Are you sure?

CAMILLE: Yes, unless you know of something else.

ALICE: Of course not.

CAMILLE: Then it's the reason.

ALICE: Then it's stupid!

CAMILLE: *(amused)* Are you calling my husband stupid?

ALICE: No, no, I am very fond of Claude, but the only reason we decided to live as one family in this house was to save us all money. If we separate, we'll be paying for separate households again.

CAMILLE: We've got no money coming in. None at all at the moment and that means Ernest is paying for two families under the one roof. Where's the economy in that for you?

ALICE: We're not two households, are we, really? We share most things.

CAMILLE: Tell me about it!

ALICE: I'm sorry Camille. Don't we give you enough privacy?

CAMILLE: Of course you do. I just mean that Claude sees Ernest paying for everything lately and it has to stop. That's why Claude has written the letter.

ALICE: Does he mean it?

CAMILLE: Yes, when he was writing it, at the time and immediately afterwards, but he could come to regret it.

ALICE: Has the letter already gone?

CAMILLE: I think so. Yesterday evening.

ALICE: That's unlucky.

CAMILLE: I thought he might have spoken to you about it. You were talking late into the night.

ALICE: He didn't mention it.

CAMILLE: Then he's probably not serious.

ALICE: Are you certain?

CAMILLE: You've some way to go in understanding my Claude. He's always doing things like this.

ALICE: Like what?

CAMILLE: Playing on sympathies. "I'm saying I could not take another franc off you" – and then he takes ten and spends it all on some stupidly expensive overripe cheese that stinks like a dead fisherman's socks.

ALICE: But you have had times when it was better.

CAMILLE: You mean when the cheese was only as strong as the fisherman's socks before he died and just after he'd taken his annual bath? It's been going on for years.

ALICE: Things weren't so bad when Claude first came to Ernest's attention as an artist.

CAMILLE: When he painted the panels for your house in Montgeron?

ALICE: Yes, pictures of geese. I loathed those panels at first.

CAMILLE: Do you hate them now?

ALICE: How can I? They've gone. I'd just started to come to terms with them when we lost everything. Bankruptcy is so brutal.

CAMILLE: I see death as a sort of bankruptcy. The Reaper comes along just like a bailiff and carts us away like we were a cheap, gaudy trinket box or a Boulle cabinet. They don't know how to discriminate between the worthless and the precious and usually they don't bother to look what you left inside. We're all the same to these Grim Reapers.

ALICE: You and Claude were so kind to us, giving us a home when you weren't exactly wealthy yourselves.

CAMILLE: No, we were only desperate then. But to be honest we've only had really hard times in 1866, 1867, 1871 and 1868. Those were the worst years but 1872 wasn't so good either – that was the year Claude tried to kill himself.

ALICE: Neither of you have talked about this before.

CAMILLE: Why should we? It was all a bit like the first, second and third Impressionist Exhibitions.

ALICE: Groundbreaking and unusual?

CAMILLE: No, all a bit daft and a bit of a flop.

ALICE: Is that how you felt about the exhibitions? Really? Underneath?

CAMILLE: I was only talking from the press and critics point-of-view. Oh, don't go looking for chinks in my loyalty Alice, because you won't find them.

ALICE: I wasn't looking.

CAMILLE: Weren't you?

ALICE: No, but about this situation with Claude, trying to take your own life is a very serious matter.

CAMILLE: Well, before your Catholic morals implode, you've probably observed he's still alive and running around the garden playing hopscotch.

ALICE: But what happened?

CAMILLE: You really care, don't you?

ALICE: I'm anxious for you both. What if he does something like it again? Who will take care of you and the children?

CAMILLE: In the future?

ALICE: It could happen again if times are very hard and he's feeling fragile.

CAMILLE: I can't help you Alice because there's no future for me. You'll just have to do your best to get the ship back on an even keel.

ALICE: Me?

CAMILLE: You'll still be around. You've got that sort of sticky quality, haven't you? I swear, if you put your hand on my arm you'd bleed me like a leech.

ALICE: Please tell me how it happened. What made Claude do it?

CAMILLE: Jean was just a baby and we got kicked out of our lodgings. That was force of habit for us I'm afraid. So Claude.... *(CAMILLE stifles a laugh)*

ALICE: ...what about Claude?

CAMILLE: The landlord gave him no time to pull on his trousers so he was put out on the street as naked as the day he entered this world.

ALICE: He must have found that quite humiliating.

CAMILLE: I think he quite enjoyed the drama of it all but then later he took it all a bit too far by jumping in the river, trying to drown himself.

ALICE: He could have died.

CAMILLE: I think the water was only two feet deep and he managed to fish himself out and trail home afterwards.

ALICE: But you'd lost your home.

CAMILLE: Oh, we'd managed to find a little room where I was installed with Jean. So back he came, all dripping wet and sorry for himself.

ALICE: Like a lost dog.

CAMILLE: That's right Alice. Just like a lost dog. We dried him off and settled him down by the fireplace.

ALICE: So at least there was a warm fire. Perhaps things were not as bad as you recall.

CAMILLE: I said by the fireplace. I didn't say there was a fire in the grate.

ALICE: He must have been sick with worry about you and Jean.

CAMILLE: Yes, he was. He always was, but writing begging letters was much more effective than grand dying gestures.

ALICE: How did he get out of it?

CAMILLE: Scrabbled up the bank.

ALICE: I meant the poverty.

CAMILLE: Another letter to Manet of course, who got us through to the end of the month. "Manet this must be the last time I ask but ask you I must!" Claude dips in and out of poverty like, like...

ALICE: ...a ladle in a pauper's soup?

CAMILLE: I was thinking of a Wilbert in a brothel.

ALICE: Camille!

CAMILLE: Lighten up Alice, the end is nigh.

ALICE: So Claude dragged himself up the bank, back from the brink of extinction.

CAMILLE: Completely soiled his trousers. I don't know why he put them back on if he knew he was going to pull a stunt like that.

ALICE: Soiled his trousers? Was he that terrified? Poor man!

CAMILLE: I meant the knees, scrabbling up the bank.

ALICE: Oh!

CAMILLE: You didn't think....?

ALICE: Certainly not, but this just tells me you must stay here, where we can keep an eye on you all.

CAMILLE: Aren't you tired of being my nurse?

ALICE: I suppose it's my nature.

CAMILLE: A mother as well. A Madonna. So many children; five, no I mean six. Ernest must be so proud of them. Every single one.

ALICE: He is.

CAMILLE: *(Poitedly)* ***Every*** one.

ALICE: Each of them, but you must be proud too. Your sons are lovely.

CAMILLE: Well, I can't compete with your record. Six and not out and here's me struggling after a pair.

ALICE: It's not your fault you can't look after Michel properly at the moment.

CAMILLE: As a proper mother should? I feel like he doesn't know me. I watch his eyes swivel round to find you when he hears your voice.

ALICE: Like I was his nursemaid, that's all.

CAMILLE: I've never known such a martyr, the way you revel in lowly positions. Anyone would think they'd coated the silver spoon with something nasty the week you were born.

ALICE: I just want to help. You were so generous to us.

CAMILLE: We've talked about that.

ALICE: I shall never ever forget. You took us in.

CAMILLE: And how many times have you taken me in Alice?

ALICE: I don't understand you Camille.

CAMILLE: I was just referring to your kindness.

ALICE: Oh.

CAMILLE: You know, your youngest son reminds me so much of Claude.

ALICE: Children often look like the strangest sort of people but then, they change all the time.

CAMILLE: Are you saying my husband looks strange?

ALICE: You know I didn't mean that.

CAMILLE: I still see Claude in his face. He's not a good looking child.

ALICE: *(laughs)* Don't you let Claude hear you saying that!

CAMILLE: Why should Claude be bothered?

ALICE: I don't think he would be. Not really.

CAMILLE: You're a good woman, I mean the way you care for us all. It must be miserable for you and the way Claude speaks to you sometimes! He forgets himself.

ALICE: He just worries about money. It makes him prickly.

CAMILLE: That and the light changing when he's half way through a work. I've told him you can't halt the movement of the day. You have to accept sunshine moves on. If you can't change nature, you should change the canvas. But where is he?

ALICE: Claude's in the garden with the children.

CAMILLE: Ah, you said! My memory's like a colander. Is he painting them?

ALICE: The children?

CAMILLE: No, the colanders. We accumulated a valuable collection over the last decade.

ALICE: Oh Camille, I don't know where you find the energy to make jokes when....

CAMILLE: ...when you're dying? When you're about to kick the bucket? I wonder what colour Claude would paint that bucket?

ALICE: ...Camille...

CAMILLE: ...to shuffle off your mortal coil. To depart this earthly life. To leave the house and leave your door key behind on the window sill for someone to lock up.

ALICE: I meant feeling unwell.

CAMILLE: Mistress of the understatement! Anyway, I did mean painting the children really.

ALICE: He tried to paint the children, but they wanted to throw a ball about. They kept moving and when they stood still, the sun had moved and he got exasperated. He looked like an octopus, all arms, as he was trying to remix his colours but he couldn't keep up. So now he's playing as well.

CAMILLE: I wish I had the strength to get up to the window to watch them.

ALICE: Shall I help you?

CAMILLE: Here, let me try.

(CAMILLE, with immense difficulty, gets up and moves toward the window. ALICE helps her and she stands propped up by ALICE looking through the window.)

CAMILLE: Ah, there they are, right there. I'd love to go and sit in the garden with them.

ALICE: We could put a chair for you in the shade. Shall I fetch Claude? I think between us we could help you down the stairs.

CAMILLE: No. I'll only go if I can walk myself down the stairs.

ALICE: You'll soon be able to but you must take proper rests in between.

CAMILLE: It won't be long now, will it? Not too many weeks.

(CAMILLE starts to move back to the chair. ALICE assists her.)

ALICE: Don't talk this nonsense. You're a young woman like me. You've got years to go.

CAMILLE: But I'm not a lioness like you. Six children!

ALICE: You'll be strong again.

CAMILLE: Claude knows it won't be long. He sat up by my bed all night.

ALICE: You had a lot of pain.

CAMILLE: And you sat with him. I could make you out. I could make both of you out in the darkness.

ALICE: I was here for a little while. Do you mind?

CAMILLE: I'm not sure. Will you be here when I die?

ALICE: You're not dying!

CAMILLE: If I was dying and I will die one day, would you be here?

ALICE: I could die first.

CAMILLE: Rubbish! Would you be here when I go?

ALICE: Would you like me to be?

CAMILLE: I just wonder who you'll be comforting; me or Claude?

ALICE: I'm here for both of you.

CAMILLE: Really?

ALICE: Really.

CAMILLE: Claude and I have navigated some very rough seas. Money, yes, but that's not all. In the beginning his family thought I was beneath him.

ALICE: You weren't beneath him. That's ridiculous.

CAMILLE: *(Mischievously)* Oh yes I was Alice. How do you think we got Jean?

ALICE: Camille! You're full of mischief, even now.

CAMILLE: Even now.

ALICE: So, whose opinion was it? A protective mother?

CAMILLE: No. It was Claude's father who objected. His mother died when he was sixteen. I'm surprised he hasn't told you that. He tells you most things.

ALICE: He did tell me; I'd just forgotten. You've had so many hardships, my dear, but you manage to stay funny and sweet about it all.

CAMILLE: Sweet? You think I'm sweet. I'm racked with poison and you think I'm sweet. My breath is poison and my stomach's stoked with hot coals. How I would have relished feeling this warm when we were cold and hungry.

ALICE: Please don't get angry when I try to comfort you.

CAMILLE: I'm not angry.

ALICE: No, you're in pain.

CAMILLE: I don't want to talk about my pain any more.

(Silence.)

CAMILLE: Where's Ernest now?

ALICE: In Paris. He'll be here by this evening.

CAMILLE: He should be like Claude, in the garden with his children. It's a shame he can't find more time to be with them.

ALICE: I expect he does his best. There's so much going on and Ernest is trying to pull things back together but the children and I are always there in the background.

CAMILLE: But do you know what's it's really like to be in the background, just to be curtains or the wall paper or even the cracked plaster on the bricks?

ALICE: If the children and I are just wallpaper then we are always there, in the room with Ernest. I suppose it's because we're women as well, Camille. It's our lot to be a constant, not an overt force.

CAMILLE: You're so stoic.

ALICE: That will be my religion.

CAMILLE: There was a moment for me, you know.

ALICE: Camille, how can you call it "a moment"? You were, you will always be "Camille, woman in a green dress".

CAMILLE: Yes, I had my moment but I was only the model after all. It could have been any woman in that green dress, in that painting. Claude could have just used a giant courgette and drawn a face on it.

ALICE: Anyone looking at that picture can see the complete engagement of the artist with his subject. In all that darkness, the green of the cloth glows and the moment is captured perfectly forever.

CAMILLE: And ever, Amen. You sound like a junior art critic. Are those your own words or are you quoting?

ALICE: When Claude was scrabbling up that river bank trying to escape the black abyss of his domestic economics, what do you think he held on to? The face of the landlord? The faces of the locals on the street laughing?

CAMILLE: He held on to his palette probably. He gave up hanging on to other specific things when he left adolescence. Alice, you know, you could get work writing speeches.

ALICE: But what kept him going while they were all sneering?

CAMILLE: Wouldn't anyone laugh at Claude's bare arse? I wouldn't blame them.

ALICE: What I'm trying to explain is that when things were at their worst, Claude must have closed his eyes and seen the woman in the green dress, green as rich as Irish moss, shimmering and keeping the blackness at bay.

CAMILLE: You've described the material of the dress gloriously; like a promising haberdasher's apprentice. But what about the woman wearing it? If I follow your line of thinking Alice, all I can see is Manet or Renoir or some other of Claude's cronies throwing him an unfurling bolt of black and green striped silk like a rope to haul himself out of the river. That isn't me. That isn't being a muse or an inspiration.

ALICE: No, you're wrong.

CAMILLE: It is true Alice. You should be honest with a dying woman. Just look what happened after that. Claude Monet's great model became a blur in the landscape. Her features are just a foggy cloud and not worth the detail.

ALICE: How can you say that? You were the focal point on the landscape.

CAMILLE: It was all about the landscape. I was just part of it like a bush or a gatepost.

ALICE: You were his most important subject.

CAMILLE: Ah, the past tense. Now there's an admission.

ALICE: What do you mean?

CAMILLE: I bought a pamphlet weeks ago. The title was "Sitting with the Dying". Shall I give it to you?

ALICE: This is so terribly morbid Camille. You're not dying. You'll be Claude's model again. You'll be better.

CAMILLE: That's exactly what the pamphlet says. Did you write it under a pseudonym? Or did you take it from under my pillow when I was sleeping and read it, hungrily, cover to cover, anticipating what comes next?

ALICE: Read what?

CAMILLE: "Sitting with the Dying". It instructs that you must always speak hopefully and it doesn't matter what lies you tell because the subject might not be here next month or next week or even tomorrow to question you?

ALICE: And what about the afterlife?

CAMILLE: It was written by an atheist.

ALICE: As a practicing Catholic I could never read a pamphlet like that.

CAMILLE: You have to understand it's all there's left for most of us. Nothing comes afterwards. The door bangs shut with me forever locked inside and Claude and the children still in the garden.

ALICE: I wish you had faith Camille.

CAMILLE: I don't and you can't change that Alice.

ALICE: So, that means we must make *now* a good time for you.

CAMILLE: Is there coffee in the house?

ALICE: Yes, and some very decent ham and bread. Shall I fetch you some? We'll all be happy to see you eat.

CAMILLE: Last night we had nothing. Was Ernest able to send some money up from Paris?

ALICE: It was Claude. He sold a painting.

CAMILLE: *(Suddenly offended and defensive)* No he didn't. He'd have told me first.

ALICE: He only got the advance last night.

CAMILLE: So, it's a commission. Is that what you were talking about, while you were both sat by the bed?

ALICE: We spoke about it, a little.

CAMILLE: *(Hurt)* He should have told me first. I'm his wife.

ALICE: You were sleeping and he didn't want to wake you.

CAMILLE: I was awake. I could hear you whispering in the darkness. I'm his wife; he should have told me first.

ALICE: Of course you are.

CAMILLE: You don't need to tell me that Alice Hoschede. I'm telling you. Why didn't you say something when I was talking about Ernest paying for everything? Why Alice? Why is it being hidden?

ALICE: I didn't mean to be offensive.

CAMILLE: You sleep with my husband then you tell me that you don't mean to be offensive. Forget the coffee and the ham!

ALICE: Camille!

(*CAMILLE laughs explosively*)

CAMILLE: But Alice can't you see the absurdity of everything you're saying? It's a good job you're not an artist like Berthe Morisot, because you've no sense of proportion or perspective.

ALICE: Please stop laughing Camille and listen to me.

CAMILLE: Your turn to be angry now.

ALICE: But you know it's not true. I don't sleep with Claude.

CAMILLE: That was why I laughed. Your religion won't let you and it protects me as well, though I wouldn't give it the time of day. But make no mistake Alice, whatever else is kept from me the strangest rumours still manage to infiltrate my sickroom like the vapours from a hot Paris street, creeping through the gap under the door and through the spaces between the floorboards. It's in the breath of visitors and the maid as well, but never quite in their actual words.

ALICE: Do you mean Rosalee? What's that girl been saying to you?

CAMILLE: It's not just Rosalee. Please don't get annoyed with her. She's young and she certainly isn't the only one.

ALICE: I wish we could afford a better maid, but of course they come and go like clockwork soldiers, just as the money comes and goes. You can't expect loyalty from them or even any good sense and they always fill their boredom with meaningless gossip. Perhaps I should dispense with Rosalee.

CAMILLE: Spoken like a true bourgeois mistress! By God Alice, you cover the full social spectrum. What a chameleon! From nursemaid to madam and back again in one fowl swoop.

ALICE: What shall I do about Rosalee?

CAMILLE: Don't get rid of her. She needs the money. The family are poorer than church mice.

ALICE: We don't pay her much. She practically pays us for being here.

CAMILLE: She likes us. Do we give her enough to eat? I couldn't stand the idea of the poor mite being hungry. You must give her everything that I don't touch.

ALICE: She eats with the children and they never go short.

CAMILLE: You care for them well, your children and mine.

ALICE: Camille, Claude sat in a chair by your bed all night.

CAMILLE: We've talked about that. Was it a problem? Was it because he was absent from yours?

ALICE: *(Frightened and betraying exasperation)* Oh why do you keep on this line? It's hurting both of us, yet you persist. I only know because I sat with him for part of the time and I've told you that. I left and went to my own bed and then I found him slumped in the chair this morning. He hadn't moved.

CAMILLE: And where is Claude now?

ALICE: Claude is in the garden.

CAMILLE: So, we have gone full circle and arrived nowhere.

ALICE: I hope we've made some progress. I hope we've dispelled these silly ideas about myself and Claude.

CAMILLE: But even if it hasn't happened already, it will happen. I can see it even if you can't.

ALICE: Oh Camille!

CAMILLE: Camille, Camille, Camille! Don't you have something more you can say to me? You are about to take my husband and my children.

ALICE: I won't take anything from you Camille.

CAMILLE: Then please don't take my children.

ALICE: Of course I wouldn't.

CAMILLE: But you can't help yourself. You're a massive all-consuming Earth Mother. You'll suck them into your warm comforting aura, like a Norwegian stove in midwinter. Your bosom's more stuffed than an English sofa and what comfort can I give them? I am no more than a stick of gristle lying in this chair.

ALICE: They will always be your children.

CAMILLE: So how long do you think that is going to last Alice? It's over as soon as I'm gone.

ALICE: They will remember you.

CAMILLE: They're too young.

ALICE: But there are so many paintings. So many pictures. You will be everywhere.

CAMILLE: And how will my children understand their mother, the disappearing woman? A woman with no taste for life? No guts. No colour. The un-incredible, unremarkable fading lady. Whiter and whiter and blurry at the edges until she becomes nothing and another face emerges from the fog and it's not mine.

ALICE: I'll ask Claude to paint you in a blaze of colour.

CAMILLE: Ah! A blaze of colour! I think Claude will paint me one more time and there'll be less of me than there ever was. Maybe scanty white clouds for a face, a mellow characterless expression just picked out in feint violet. My children will just about see me through a blizzard and how tiresome it'll be to try and focus your memories on that.

(Below a door bangs)

ALICE: Someone's come in. I wonder who?

CAMILLE: Claude?

ALICE: Could be any of the children. Or Rosalee or Ernest if he got the early train.

CAMILLE: You go down and look Alice.

ALICE: Do you want me to bring anything when I come back up?

CAMILLE: Yes, bring me my children but then tell Claude I'm sleeping. Send him to the lower field. You said the cornflowers are beautiful there and he wouldn't want to miss the colours.

ALICE: I won't be long.

CAMILLE: No Claude wouldn't want to miss the colours.

ALICE: I promise I won't be long.

(Lights long fade, during which we hear the voices of CLAUDE and ALICE MONET off.)

CLAUDE MONET: *(off)* So, where was I while you two had this conversation?

ALICE MONET: *(off)* You were in the garden Claude.

CLAUDE MONET: *(off)* She was very cruel to you Alice.

ALICE MONET: *(off)* But life was cruel to her then and in the end she was right, wasn't she?

CLAUDE MONET: *(off)* I wouldn't let it haunt you anymore. There's nothing to be done. Where did you say I was Alice?

ALICE MONET: *(off)* In the garden Claude, in the garden.

The End

The Arrival of Dead Dick's Box

All life is an experiment.
The more experiments you make
the better.
-Ralph Waldo Emerson

Synopsis

A comedy drama in one act and in one domestic setting.

Fussy health and safety consultant, Lewis, receives a mysterious box. It is addressed to himself and two friends, Caroline and Jan, whom he urgently summons to his flat. Caroline arrives first. She is a hairdresser and it suits her to play dumb although she is rather more intelligent than it seems. Lewis explains that a box has arrived for them from Dick, a friend of all three who disappeared a year ago. Jan, who is Dutch and runs a paintballing business, arrives soon afterwards. While Lewis answers the door to him, Caroline faints thinking Dick has died and his ashes have been sent to them.

Now all are assembled, Lewis reads the accompanying letter written by Dick. It is an apology for leaving so suddenly, for not being in touch and for being a poor friend. They proceed to open the box and unwrap the contents; a bar of soap, a small souvenir clog, a shuttlecock and a pair of pliers.

The friends continue to discuss what the four items signify and what their missing friend is trying to say to them. They take their task seriously and explore some of their more unsavoury memories of Dick. Tensions between the three, however, rise to the surface and apparent truths are revealed. Jan thinks Lewis is ridiculously anal-retentive and unimaginative, while Lewis views Jan as a macho oaf. Caroline suspects they both view her as "rather thick" and neither chooses to deny this. Unfortunately, they only chose share their more sympathetic views of each other with the audience.

After Jan challenges Lewis to pull out his fingernail with the pliers and Caroline leaves in a huff, Lewis is left alone. He goes to his kitchen leaving the audience to hear a radio news report about that theft of items from an art installation at the Tate Gallery which include...a bar of soap, a clog, a shuttlecock and a pair of pliers. Clearly Dick is a joker!

Cast

LEWIS – male, a health and safety consultant
JAN - male, Dutch, runs a paintball business
CAROLINE – female, hairstylist with own business

All characters are of the same generation and may be aged anywhere between 30 and 50 years approximately.

This play was first performed by "The Corner House Group", Worksop in February 2011.

(The interior of LEWIS'S flat, which includes a small dining room table, three chairs and behind, a sideboard or side table, on which stands a radio. The radio is playing classical music as the scene starts. On the middle of the dining table is a box wrapped in brown paper and beside it, a white envelope. LEWIS sits at the table looking at the box. He picks it up, shakes it gently and then puts it down on the table again. He picks it up again, puts it to his ear and listens, but there is nothing to hear. He puts the box down, pushes his chair back from the table and examines it from a greater distance. He moves toward the table again and smells the box. He sighs. There are no clues. He folds his arms and just looks at the box. There is a knock at the door. LEWIS gets up, turns off the radio and exits to answer the door.)

CAROLINE: *(off)* Where is he?

(Enter CAROLINE, followed by LEWIS. LEWIS indicates the box on the table.)

CAROLINE: Oh bugger, it's a box.

LEWIS: Well yes, it's box-shaped and made of cardboard. I took it to be a box but it does have one special feature.

CAROLINE: Special feature?

LEWIS: It rattles when you shake it.

CAROLINE: This isn't what I expected.

LEWIS: It's a complete surprise for all of us.

CAROLINE: Does Jan know?

LEWIS: I 'phoned Jan, straight after I 'phoned you. He won't be long.

CAROLINE: I was with a client when you called.

LEWIS: I'm sorry. I thought you'd want to know straightaway.

CAROLINE: The tongs weren't hot enough and I had to rush her off half cock.

LEWIS: Rush who off?

CAROLINE: My client.

LEWIS: You could have waited. I only said "as soon as you can", not "immediately". It's not my fault you're so jumpy.

CAROLINE: You called me at work! I thought it was urgent so she's gone out with bends instead of Regency ringlets and all for this. A box.

LEWIS: I don't see the problem.

CAROLINE: She was a wedding booking! Well Hen Night actually. But don't you get it? Even I take pride in my work. I ask you, a bride with bends!

LEWIS: Easily cured, if you can find a hyperbaric unit.

CAROLINE: What? What are you on about? What's the big word for?

LEWIS: Never mind. The important thing is that you switched off the tongs before you left. I'm assuming you did.

CAROLINE: What dimension are you in Lewis? I'm talking art and you're talking...

LEWIS: ...Health and safety. It's the first dimension. You won't move to the second dimension without it.

CAROLINE: My reputation will be shredded and all for this flamin' box.

LEWIS: I thought nothing could shake the reputation of "International Hair by Caroline Crispin".

CAROLINE: Don't you believe it.

LEWIS: It's hair for goodness sake! You wash it and that's it; curls, colour and whatever else you've tampered with, all gone, washed away down the plug hole.

CAROLINE: You couldn't be more wrong Lewis.

LEWIS: I suppose if you had an accident, I mean bad enough to get the Health and Safety Executive in, now that would be pretty permanent. Kaput! Not many small businesses can bounce back from that.

CAROLINE: It only ever works on one level, doesn't it Lewis, your mind?

LEWIS: It's called "being thorough". Isn't the care and well-being of your customers important to you Caroline?

CAROLINE: No, their hair is.

LEWIS: Is there nothing deeper?

CAROLINE: That's where my reputation rests. I may as well send them all out with a free batch of nits with every cut and finish. *(afterthought)* The cut would be stunning, naturally.

LEWIS: Naturally.

CAROLINE: What are we all here for anyway? A box and no Dick? I was sure you said on the 'phone Dick was here; I was hoping for flesh, blood and a stupid malevolent grin, not brown paper and cardboard.

LEWIS: I didn't say he was actually here, but I suppose, in a manner of speaking, he is.

CAROLINE: What do you mean by that Lewis? I thought you said...

(Loud knocking at the door.)

LEWIS: ..That's Jan. I'll let him in.

(Exit LEWIS. CAROLINE sits at the table looking at the box. Gingerly, she picks it up, shakes it gently and then puts it down on the table again. She picks it up again, puts it to her ear and listens, but there is nothing to hear. She smells it, but this gives no clues. She puts the box down and looks at it in a very worried way.)

CAROLINE: *(with a sudden realisation and panic)* Lewis! This box Lewis......

LEWIS: *(off)* Hang on. I'm letting Jan in.

CAROLINE: *(weakly)* But I know about the box. Oh my God, Lewis, it can't be. Didn't he realise?

(She stands up, deeply shaken, leaning against the table, horrified at what she is thinking. She clasps her hands to her mouth as though she is about to vomit, but then she collapses to the floor in a faint. Enter LEWIS and JAN.)

JAN: Caroline!

(JAN immediately gets down on his knees to start First Aid procedures. He checks her airways, breathing and then he gently shakes her shoulders.)

JAN: Caroline. *(To LEWIS:)* She's out like a light.

LEWIS: What's the matter with her?

JAN: Fainted maybe. Caroline! Caroline!

(CAROLINE groans as she starts to gain consciousness.)

JAN: She's coming round. *(To CAROLINE:)* Caroline, it's Jan. I'm putting you in the recovery position. Try to stay calm.

LEWIS: Head between her knees.

JAN: Heads between knees is for feeling faint. It's not the recovery position.

(Jan skilfully turns CAROLINE onto her side.)

LEWIS: *(Quietly turning away)* Smart arse!

JAN: Just lie still for a moment.

LEWIS: I wonder what caused that.

JAN: How can I say? I wasn't here.

LEWIS: And I was opening the door to you.

JAN: Must have been something you said - or did - Lewis.

LEWIS: She was only here for a couple of minutes before you came.

JAN: So, what happened?

LEWIS: She was talking about one of her clients. I did nothing to her.

JAN: Okay! Okay! You always think I'm accusing you of something.

LEWIS: That's because you are. And didn't you just say I must have done something? I heard it with my own ears. She may well have been poorly before she came here.

JAN: Perhaps she just had a bad shock.

LEWIS: Everything's been "Portable Appliance Tested" in the last three months. That's PAT Testing to those of us in the profession. *(JAN casts his heavenwards and tuts.)* I've put labels on all plugs and power supplies. You know, you couldn't be safer than in here and I am emphatically certain that Caroline has not had a shock.

JAN: I didn't mean that. The return of Dick is enough to bring anyone toppling down.

(CAROLINE tries to sit up suddenly with panic.)

JAN: Hey, steady now.

CAROLINE: That box…

(*CAROLINE tries to both rise and point to the parcel on the table at the same time.*)

LEWIS: What about it?

JAN: What box?

CAROLINE: The box on the table. I know what it is and it's terrible.

JAN: Don't worry about the box. Do you think old Lewis is hiding a bomb in there?

CAROLINE: No, it's Dick!

JAN: Do you think she knocked her head when she fell?

LEWIS: No, you usually go limp when you faint in my experience.

JAN: Do much fainting, do you Lewis?

LEWIS: We covered it on the First Aid Diploma.

JAN: She may have slipped and tensed up. That's how it usually happens.

CAROLINE: Stop talking about me.

LEWIS: What would she have slipped on, may I ask? There's an anti-slip runner all around the edge of the rug and if the floor was wet, I'd put a sign out. Well, I wouldn't have if it was just me; I'm not anal retentive you know, but when people come round, I do. But I wasn't here to witness it, remember? I was out there.

(*CAROLINE struggles to rise again.*)

CAROLINE: Dick's in the box!

LEWIS: No, he isn't Caroline. What on earth….

CAROLINE: ...You said Dick was here and the only way he could be here, in that box, is if he'd changed shape in some way?

(CAROLINE is now on her feet and staggers to the table. JAN and LEWIS start to laugh)

JAN: And what do you think Dick would have transformed into? A squid?

LEWIS: *(smugly)* A "Grow your own Dinosaur on the Kitchen Windowsill" kit?

JAN: A deep fat fryer?

LEWIS: I'd have them banned. Cause of too many accidents.

CAROLINE: *(Getting cross)* No, ashes! Dick could fit in the box if he was ashes.

LEWIS: You're sucking the wrong end of the pencil Caroline.

CAROLINE: No, can't you see it? Dick's dead and we've been sent his ashes because we're his best friends.

JAN: It is possible. She could be right.

(JAN and LEWIS start to laugh again.)

LEWIS: No, she's not. You know what she's like – going off at a complete tangent and misunderstanding everything. She's always doing it.

CAROLINE: Huh! I'm not!

(JAN and CAROLINE freeze.)

LEWIS: *(to audience:)* I first saw Caroline when I was sixteen. I was thinking of Fine Art in those days and a group of us had been taken to the Art College for a look around. Anyway, one of the lecturers was talking to us on the stairs when this party from another school was brought into the vestibule below. They had to stand there for a bit because we were in the way, wearing those sneering hostile looks that happen when different schools encounter one another, particularly when they have on their avant-garde best and we were in our blazers. She was at the back of the huddle and from my higher angle; well her cheekbones looked fantastic; just like a

Russian model. I hung around for a bit and tried to talk to her but then she opened her mouth and told me to "f-ing sod off". Just like that. Now, I don't think she can remember it at all. Oh, I did apply for that Art College but they told me to "f-ing sod off" as well.

(JAN and CAROLINE unfreeze.)

JAN: I've always found her straightforward. Simple.

CAROLINE: Simple! And the alternative is to be a pedantic bottom wipe like Lewis!

LEWIS: For Dick's sake, I'll ignore that Caroline. I know you're not feeling well and probably don't know what "pedantic" means.

CAROLINE: I own a dictionary!

JAN: I've seen it.

LEWIS: Okay. Okay. Will you sit down Jan? And both of you give me the chance to make a rational explanation please!

(JAN sits at the table.)

JAN: Are you feeling all right now Caroline?

CAROLINE: I picked him up you know. I've never touched a dead body. Have either of you two?

LEWIS: Are you going to let me explain this?

JAN: You like being in control, don't you Lewis?

LEWIS: The parcel was sent to this address. I don't choose leadership. Leadership has chosen me, tapped me on the shoulder, prodded me in the ribs.

JAN: Like a fly landing on your toast and jam and not being able to free its feet?

LEWIS: If you must put it that way.

CAROLINE: He was so hefty when he was alive but he doesn't weigh more than a value pack of cornflakes now. Poor Dick.

JAN: It's the spirit weighing us down. None of us weigh much, once the spirit has left our body.

CAROLINE: So, at Weight Watchers they think they're dealing with blubber and they're really tackling the human spirit?

JAN: That's profound.

CAROLINE: Thank you.

JAN: You should write it down.

(JAN and LEWIS freeze)

CAROLINE: *(to audience)* It's a game. Jan doesn't mean it. We both know it was a weak attempt at being clever, but what's really important is that Jan doesn't twig that I understand. I hide behind not being very clever. It gives you the chance to look at people and see what they reveal about themselves. They don't think they have to impress you; just throw a cheap line and expect you to be satisfied. But I don't like being short changed and one day I'll get around to telling Jan that. All these years he's really been patronising Einstein the Hairdresser and he doesn't know it.

(JAN and LEWIS unfreeze)

LEWIS: *(firmly)* Come on, let me run through this. Let me explain to both of you.

CAROLINE: We're listening.

LEWIS: Firstly, on the telephone I said, "There's something here from Dick", which is quite different to "Dick's here". Now, an hour ago this parcel, this box, was delivered by a courier and with it came this letter.

(LEWIS picks up the envelope and flaps it about.)

JAN: You've opened the letter?

LEWIS: Of course I opened it. How would I have known that it had come from Dick and that I had to 'phone you two?

CAROLINE: Imagine, being able to post your own ashes home to your friends.

LEWIS: I thought I'd put paid to that idea.

JAN: Caroline, I think it's a parcel from Dick. It's not actually Dick.

CAROLINE: I know that now! I was just commenting on a business opportunity.

JAN: Could be a profitable sideline in your salon.

CAROLINE: I'll think about it.

JAN: So Lewis, what did it say on the envelope?

LEWIS: The letter? *(Reading:)* "To Jan, Caroline..."

JAN: ...that's what it says?

LEWIS: That's what I said.

JAN: "And Lewis". *(With irony)* I understand. Not Lewis, Jan and Caroline or Lewis, Caroline and Jan, it said to Jan, Caroline and *also* Lewis.

LEWIS: Split hairs if you must.

JAN: That's Caroline's job.

CAROLINE: As if ?!...

LEWIS: ...Very smart! I'll read the letter to you.

JAN: Because of course, Caroline and I can't read.

LEWIS: You can read it yourself!

CAROLINE: Please read it Lewis. If Dick is dead...

(JAN groans.)

LEWIS: Dick is not dead! *(LEWIS reads the letter)* "Dear Jan, Caroline and Lewis" *(JAN clears his throat meaningfully)* "It's a year today since I left and I bet you're having a party to celebrate a full twelve months without me. LOL! I didn't give any of you a reason for going. In fact, I think it's quite probable I forgot to tell any of you I was leaving anyway. I know you'll be sitting there slagging me off and saying it's not how a friend should carry on. With this letter, and to make up for my below average "friending" skills, you'll get a box. The insides will give you something to remember me by if I don't return. Cheers! Dick."

JAN: Just like Dick.

LEWIS: The punctuation's all wrong. He hasn't used one capital letter.

JAN: What's in the box?

LEWIS: I don't know.

JAN: I would have thought you'd taken responsibility – in your leadership role.

LEWIS: When I read the letter, it was implied that we should all open the box together.

CAROLINE: What does he mean? "If I never return?" Do you think he's going to die?

JAN: Well, we've made progress. Caroline had Dick dead and now he's only dying.

LEWIS: I think we should take it at face value.

JAN: I think we should open it first and see what's in there.

CAROLINE: This is weird. Let's get it over with.

JAN: Do you know what's in there Lewis?

LEWIS: I've told you. I've no idea.

JAN: Are you sure you weren't tempted to take a little preview, in your leadership role?

LEWIS: Grow up Jan! The barbed inferences are getting us nowhere.

JAN: I wonder why?

CAROLINE: Just open it Lewis.

(LEWIS tries to peel the tape off the box, which is difficult.)

LEWIS: Caroline, have you got your hairdressing scissors with you?

CAROLINE: You are joking! My scissors, the tools of my art, to hack at Sellotape? I keep them razor sharp for a precision finish and what do you think Sellotape will do to that?

LEWIS: The sharper they are, the safer they are.

(JAN gets a large pen knife from his pocket and passes it to LEWIS.)

LEWIS: Thank you.

(LEWIS cuts through the tape and opens the box. They all lean forward to peer in the box and then look at one another. LEWIS carefully lifts four small parcels wrapped in newspaper and places them on the table.)

CAROLINE: Is that all?

JAN: They could be anything. Emeralds, shiitake mushrooms or Dick could have just wrapped up his pooh this morning and posted it to us.

CAROLINE: Please!

(CAROLINE and LEWIS freeze.)

JAN: (to audience) Lewis gets a lot of headaches and takes too many paracetomel. It's funny because he's so careful in every other aspect of his life, but one day I think he'll overdo it. It's all stress and too much work. He's got two jobs. I've known him have three jobs at once. Never stops working. His only parent, his father, died when

Lewis was nineteen and he fought with every part of his self to keep his two younger brothers together and with him. He's still putting the younger one through university and the other, doesn't do much to help himself. He married young, twice I think, kids all over the place and always he's got his hand out to Lewis. Lewis never says "no". I really should stop baiting him, but he's such a soft target and so easy to lay your hands on.

(*CAROLINE and LEWIS unfreeze*)

LEWIS: What do we do now?

JAN: Unwrap them and pray it's not Dick's droppings.

CAROLINE: Where do we start?

JAN: You pick one Caroline.

CAROLINE: Er...that one.

(*CAROLINE points to one of the parcels, which LEWIS unwraps. He places the contents on the table. It is a bar of soap. JAN starts to laugh.*)

CAROLINE: Is that it?

LEWIS: It seems meagre.

JAN: What did you really expect? A gold bar?

LEWIS: Well, it doesn't make sense, after all this bother; a bar of vegetable soap.

CAROLINE: Perhaps it's a mistake. Perhaps he meant to put something else in.

JAN: The situation's improving Caroline. At least you think Dick is alive and kicking.

CAROLINE: He'll get a kicking if he's caused all this trouble just for that.

LEWIS: Well if it was intended, it doesn't mean much.

JAN: Why should it mean anything? A bar of soap is a bar of soap.

CAROLINE: And highlights are highlights and eighty quid is eighty quid. I've got a customer waiting.

LEWIS: Can't you stop a bit longer while we get our heads around this. We were obviously all meant to be assembled and I'd prefer to do this properly.

CAROLINE: The only person who needs to get his head around this is Dick. He was a dirty old sod at the best of times. Did you ever see Dick have a wash?

LEWIS: Not that I recall. His hygiene was questionable.

CAROLINE: Questionable? He used to stink. He even stank worse than Jan. It was like a badger with a hormone imbalance.

JAN: Much appreciated Caroline.

CAROLINE: Well, you've got an excuse, rolling about in the woods all day, but Dick ronked. Friend or no friend I'll say it; Dick and detergent never did have a close relationship.

JAN: But Dick didn't know that. He just thought the way he smelt was normal.

CAROLINE: Normal! It was disgusting! If Dick sent us a bar of soap, it's because he thinks it was a new innovation and he was trying to be nice by letting us in on it. I can see him shoving his jack plug in the side and not understanding why it doesn't play music. Then he'd start his moaning: "Oh, Apple have really messed up this with this twelfth generation I-Tablet. No wireless connection".

JAN: Maybe he thinks we all stink. Perhaps he wants us to use the soap?

LEWIS: Don't be facetious. There must be more to it.

JAN: Five minutes ago we were supposed to take it "at face value".

LEWIS: I'm talking about looking at the evidence. Dick has not so much as emailed any one of us for a year, then he goes to the trouble of paying a courier to bring us a bar of soap. Answer that, will you?

CAROLINE: Well, I can't see it.

JAN: You answer it Lewis. You explain what you think is going on here.

CAROLINE: Yea, take us to the next dimension Lewis.

JAN: Have you got enough time Caroline? We'll have to wait while he completes a risk assessment form.

(LEWIS stands and starts to pace.)

LEWIS: You two are just time wasters. You act like a couple of kids.

CAROLINE: I really mean it Lewis. I want to know what you're driving at.

LEWIS: Okay, if you're serious, I'm not sure but I think it's a message.

(CAROLINE picks up the bar of soap and reads what is printed on it.)

CAROLINE: It says: "Cucumber and Comfrey Pure Vegetable Oil Soap. Hand made in Boston, Lincs."

JAN: Perhaps Dick works in soap making now. Electrical engineer to soap works; a predictable and Dick–like career move I'd say. Of course, he might have been headhunted by the cosmetics industry.

LEWIS: No, it's more than a bar of soap. It's a symbol.

JAN: Of what? The cleansing of a filthy mind?

LEWIS: That's too simple... *(ruminating:)*...but you're on the right track with "cleansing" though.

JAN and CAROLINE: What?

LEWIS: Dick's trying to tell us he's changed. In some way he's been cleansed.

JAN: In your next breath you'll be saying that Dick has joined the church.

CAROLINE: Dick used to vomit if he was forced to walk past a church.

LEWIS: Try to stay in the rounds of reality Caroline.

CAROLINE: It's true! I've been with him when it happened.

LEWIS: Rubbish.

CAROLINE: Just the sight of the spire over the tree tops would have him heaving. He'd try to get it in the bushes but it didn't always manage it. Once, it landed on my shoe. I was pretty livid but Dick said to pretend it was a new sort of appliqué.

LEWIS: Well, it doesn't have to be the church. It doesn't even have to be religion, but perhaps he's telling us he's a new Dick.

(JAN laughs sneeringly.)

CAROLINE: I think we should open another one.

(CAROLINE and JAN freeze)

LEWIS: *(to audience)* What's that saying? "Remember, some people are only living because you're not allowed to kill them". That's right up there with, "Don't wish for everything unless you have a very big cupboard". Words of pure undiluted wisdom, at least in my view. *(Change of tone to anger)* If I had an axe, I'd kill Jan. Take his bloody head off. Oh, it would cause a mess I know and I don't like mess. That's probably the only thing that's ever stopped me.

(CAROLINE and JAN unfreeze)

CAROLINE: You choose this time Jan.

JAN: Does it matter which one we open next?

LEWIS: I'll choose then.

(LEWIS selects another parcel and unwraps it. Inside is a small wooden clog marked " Souvenir from Amsterdam".)

CAROLINE: Well, it's obvious isn't it? It's a Dutch clog. Jan?

JAN: Why should it have anything to do with me?

LEWIS: As Caroline said, "Dutch" or have you changed your nationality since we last spoke?

JAN: It says "Souvenir of Amsterdam". I'm not from Amsterdam and I've never been there. You both know my family moved to Germany when I was nine years old.

CAROLINE: What? You must have been to Amsterdam. It's your capital city.

JAN: You are not obliged to visit your capital city. I have never been to Amsterdam and what's more, Dick knew that.

CAROLINE: Perhaps he's telling you that he thinks you should go there. I've been. So has Dick. It's full of performance artists and sex shops.

LEWIS: (*Pointing to the clog*) Not the sort of thing you find in sex shops, at least not the sort....

JAN: ...yes Lewis?

CAROLINE: Can you imagine anything less sexy? Nice fifties kitsch though. This is the sort of thing you'd chuck out and then they say it's collectable.

JAN: I always wonder who *they* are, this group of people who decide suddenly that something is valuable.

LEWIS: We're thinking too widely here. We just need to "think Dick".

JAN: So you "think Dick" and we'll try and work out why he sent us a clog.

LEWIS: You never stop to consider what anything represents. Perhaps, Dick is saying that he is capable of depravity.

CAROLINE: Not half! Dick couldn't say hello to me without asking me what colour knickers I was wearing.

LEWIS: And he was honest about that. He knew himself like he probably knew Amsterdam; a city of depravity, low and cheap but also the city of Anne Frank – noble, resilient and cheerful.

CAROLINE: It's just not right. No one can talk about Anne Frank and Dick in the same room, let alone the same breath. I will chuck up.

JAN: You've already passed out. Get a nose bleed and you'll have the hat trick of human malfunctions.

CAROLINE: You make me sound like a photocopier.

LEWIS: Are you both without an imagination?

CAROLINE: Hey, there's a label on the bottom of this clog. It says "Made in England". See Jan, right there.

LEWIS: It makes no difference. The intention of the maker was to represent a Dutch clog and that is what it is. The world is not as straightforward as "Made in England" labels. It's full of layers and conflicts and textures. You two, your thinking puts me mind of a sheet of impenetrable white Formica.

CAROLINE: Were we talking about your kitchen?

JAN: Lewis, I can't believe you can lecture anyone on imagination? You, Health and Safety Consultant extraordinaire, whose very existence seems to be to find rules and stumbling blocks for every form of physical activity the human race is capable of.

LEWIS: You're a short-sighted fool Jan. Health and Safety does not control the gymnastics of the mind. My imagination knows no limit but my professionalism ensures that people are not curtailed by a stupid-bloody-accident that defeats imagination, physicality and can lead to foreshortened mortality.

CAROLINE: That was almost poetical Lewis; I feel moved and impressed.

LEWIS: Really? Do you?

CAROLINE: I read poetry sometimes. I like "The Lady of Shalott".

LEWIS: I know the rest of the population likes to think that people in my line of work have narrowed and choked up gullies for minds, but it just isn't true. It's unbelievably imaginative. Do you know that sometimes when I'm sitting at my desk at work, or sometimes when I'm on my own here in the evening, I close my eyes and it all runs like a film. *(With great feeling)* Extreme close up on the banister. There's a screw coming out of the fitting. It falls, rolls away, and skitters down the side of the stair where it's uncarpeted. Cut to old lady, rather overweight, her point of view coming down the stairs in cheap, thin-soled slippers. The carpet is a manmade fibre so medium shot on the inevitable slip. Camera pulls back as she falls down the stairs grasping for the banister, which she finds and as her hand snatches heavily for it, back to the close-up of the fitting. Between the weight of the women and the want of a screw, the fitting is wrenched dramatically from the wall and down the stairs she plummets. Overhead shot pulls out as she lies sprawled at the foot of the hallway. The postman calls; we can see his outline through the frosted glass of the front door and several letters cascade poignantly onto her prone body. The postman moves on, unaware of the tragedy that lies beyond the letterbox. Pure art. *(He relaxes from the intensity of speech to an assured tone.)* That's the sort of tiny detail I always draw their attention to when I'm doing a consultation - all for the want of a screw, hey?

CAROLINE: That's horrible Lewis!

JAN: It's bull! You want imagination? Okay, ignore the writing, "Souvenir from Amsterdam", because that's a red herring. *(Rapidly and dramatically)* It is, in reality, the clog from the foot of a mill girl in mid-nineteenth century Lancashire, hardworking and optimistic. She never understands there's no future, no real potential for her other than the life of slave to the bulging pockets of a greedy industrialist, who in turn is a slave to buying starch for the lace petticoats of his over-embellished and spoilt poodle of a wife. And the mill girl, you can hear her clogs ringing out plaintively on the cobbles as she strides wearily home through the dark streets to her scanty scrag end of mutton supper. That's imagination. Maybe, that's what Dick wanted us to think about.

LEWIS: I doubt it. You've just described a collection of clichés. Been plundering Elizabeth Gaskell, have we?

JAN: And you weren't full of Hitchcockian clichés a moment ago? What I can say is that I probably know more about the history of your culture than you know about mine.

CAROLINE: Bloody hell. To think you waste your life running a paint ball business. Who's this girl you're talking about anyway? Did Dick know her?

LEWIS: Paint balling! Pandering to innate aggression! Facilitating it! If I put my mind to it, I could have you closed down. I know the rules you contravene.

JAN: And there's Lewis's imagination for you! "I'll have you closed down." He's shown his true essence.

CAROLINE: I liked your story Jan. I never thought about Dick as romantic in his thoughts.

JAN: And I never thought of Dick as Anne Frank. Oh Caroline! It's everything that Dick would not think about. Shall we stop being fantastical now and open another parcel?

LEWIS: (Grimly) Yes, let's move on.

(LEWIS picks up another parcel and unwraps it. It's a shuttlecock. CAROLINE picks it up.)

CAROLINE: I used to like a game of badminton. Here catch!

(CAROLINE tosses the shuttlecock across to the table to JAN like a missile, who throws it back. They quickly fall into an enjoyable rhythm of throwing it back and forth. LEWIS rises from the table, thrusts his hands in his pockets and walks away.)

LEWIS: We haven't had a chance to examine it yet.

CAROLINE: Examine it? Is it taking its GCSEs?

LEWIS: You know. Look at it properly.

CAROLINE: Here Lewis. Join in.

(She throws the shuttlecock to LEWIS. After a little hesitation he throws it to JAN. JAN throws it to LEWIS and now Caroline is forced to watch.)

CAROLINE: I understand this one. I know what it means.

JAN: Yes. Dick's joined a health club.

LEWIS: Beyond the bounds of reality or imagination.

CAROLINE: I'm being serious. Didn't Dick ever tell you guys about his childhood? Dick's parents split up and he used to say to me that he was shunted back and forth between them "like a shuttlecock".

JAN: I understand. To each parent he was like a metaphor for an overdue bill and they couldn't wait to get him off their hands. I'd do the same if I'd sired Dick.

LEWIS: You've got a cruel streak.

JAN: Domestic reality is the cruellest.

LEWIS: Do you know the history of the shuttlecock?

JAN: They used to be made of feathers and cork. Now they're plastic.

LEWIS: There's more to it than it. We look at a shuttlecock and we all think of whacking it between two rackets but it's thousands of years old and a beast in its own right. They played it a bit like football in China, but now it's more like volleyball. Agility, concentration, they've even used it in military training.

(LEWIS and JAN freeze)

CAROLINE: *(to audience)* He looks so much younger and less, I don't know, less painful when he's really enthusiastic about something. I just want to give him a hug and talk to him about Jean-Paul Satre and the Rowntree Foundation and "The Archers".

(LEWIS and JAN unfreeze)

LEWIS: There two types of shuttlecock; the artistic game and team play, but either way you're not allowed to touch it with your hands but you have to keep it in the air. You know, it's popular again and it's played all over the world; Brazil, Singapore, the US, Indonesia, Greece, France. They're some real pioneers in bringing it into the modern age. I know all the moves; leopard head, dragon tail, sitting tiger, standing crane, flying dragon, snake kick.

JAN: I suppose you play this sport Lewis? You seem to know a ridiculous amount of detail.

LEWIS: I picked it up at after Christmas. They've just started sessions at the leisure club and we're forming a team.

CAROLINE: You've never brought it up before.

LEWIS: Well, I didn't think it would interest you, knowing how you like to take the rip. It's strange that Dick should know. It's the only reason he's sent the shuttlecock, surely?

CAROLINE: I don't know about that, but sounds a lot of fuss about bugger all to me. Give me the two bats and a bit of moulded plastic any day.

LEWIS: I suppose you both think paint balling is superior.

JAN: You've never tried, have you Lewis?

LEWIS: You play in fantasy land Jan; I'll get on with reality.

JAN: I don't play.

LEWIS: You create other people's fairy tale battles in your forest playground. I've seen all those aggressive bands of little runty-types who pay what, fifty or sixty quid, so you can make them feel big with a gun in their hands.

CAROLINE: Don't start Lewis. I've been paint balling and I enjoyed it.

JAN: Dick came once.

CAROLINE: Yea, he did and he was useless. Thank God he was on the other team; we annihilated him. You couldn't see him in the end, he was like one of those artist's boards...

JAN: Palettes?

CAROLINE: Yea, palettes. Just a mass of different coloured paint splats.

LEWIS: You won't convince me that it's anything other than a game for big kids.

JAN: Says the man tossing the shuttlecock. You should try it Lewis. It's not just playing with a weapon. It's the whole forest environment. You are dissolved into nature. The forest becomes your friend, your camouflage, your challenge.

CAROLINE: The first time I did it, I was cut off from my team and I was waiting for them to find me. I lay on my front in this deep bracken and kept my head down. Then I heard the other team coming and I started to tremble all over, shaking like a French stick in the front basket of an Italian scooter. You forget it's just a game. I kept forcing myself hard into the ground, trying to disappear. My heart was like a Kango Hammer striking a man-hole cover. I knew I was shaking the ground and they'd feel the vibrations through their feet. Then, after a minute or two I realised they hadn't seen me and were going away. I was still shaking, more than ever, every finger, every eyelash. I just couldn't keep still. Then I thought I could calm myself down by breathing deeply and just concentrating on a few blades of grass in front of me. I was still lying on the ground you see. The grass was very still and I thought if I just looked at it hard, it would help me become still.

LEWIS: And this sort of adrenalin rush is meant to be good for you?

CAROLINE: The thing is that for the first time I saw that the grass was more than one shade of green. I always thought it was just one colour before that. And you know what? That difference in the tones gave me the idea for the colours I used in that competition.

JAN: When you went to Portugal?

CAROLINE: *(Proudly:)* Yea, when I won in Portugal.

LEWIS: You won a hairdressing competition by dying someone's hair different shades of grass green?

CAROLINE: Yes, exactly, the different tones inspired me; the difference between one side of the blade and the other. To top it off, I cut the tips of my model's hair in the shape of the tips of grass. It was revolution. That's when I became international. "International Hair by Caroline Crispin". The name was Dick's idea.

LEWIS: Good old Dick!

CAROLINE: I was entitled. It was an international competition so I am allowed to call the business that without misleading anyone. I know some people laugh and say behind my back "How can you have international hair?" but they could ask, "How did you become international Caroline?" Anyway, it's a marketing triumph and it gets me noticed. When you're just ordinary like you and me, you have to grab any chance you can to come into the spotlight or the rest of the world tramples over you like you didn't exist. One day, I "googled" my name and nothing came back. That tells you that you never happened, doesn't it? So I had to find a way to make a mark and now my appointment book is full.

JAN: There is nothing wrong with the name of your business Caroline.

CAROLINE: I just wish I had the guts to pretend I can live up to it and be as big as the name sounds. But I've lost the plot, haven't I? I was only trying to tell Lewis that if I hadn't gone paint balling I wouldn't have got the idea and won that competition. That's all. I wouldn't have seen the colours. You have to have new experiences.

LEWIS: *(gently)* But Caroline, you could have seen the variations in the colour of grass anywhere; walking in the park or on a picnic. Easiest of all, buy a book on the Pre-Raphaelites. It could happen anywhere there's grass.

JAN: But it didn't.

CAROLINE: Jan's right you know. It was only because I was wound up and straining my head for something to be normal and found out that normal wasn't what I thought it was. Normal isn't normal, is it?

(A moment's silence.)

LEWIS: There's still the last parcel to open.

JAN: You're the boss.

(They all return to the table and sit. LEWIS opens the last parcel. It is a pair of pliers.)

CAROLINE: Very useful.

JAN: For whom?

CAROLINE: I don't know.

LEWIS: Pliers. They're like all tools. You need to know what you're doing.

JAN: Everything you say reverberates with fear. You wouldn't use a drinking straw without a three-part training course.

LEWIS: *(in a tired way)* Get off my back.

CAROLINE: Can't we talk about anything without you two knocking lumps off one another?

LEWIS: Come on Caroline. Even you can see he provokes me. He makes a hobby of it.

JAN: You let yourself be provoked.

LEWIS: I do not!

JAN: Perhaps it's just guilt because you're constantly trying to fence us in with your safety-conscious thinking. Everything you say. Everything you think. It's all so safe. You can't even take up a sport that's not been tried and tested over thousands of years.

CAROLINE: I wish you could both stop being vile. I'm not enjoying this you know.

LEWIS: It's not all fun and games Caroline.

JAN: When was it ever Lewis?

CAROLINE: If I think about it, I haven't enjoyed being in the same room as you two together since…since…

JAN: …since Dick left.

LEWIS: We're only here because of Dick. You don't think I would just sit here and let Jan call me a coward if there wasn't good reason to be here. I'm not a coward.

JAN: Do something to prove otherwise.

LEWIS: What? Paint balling?

JAN: You see these *(toying with the pliers)*, imagine that Dick sent them...

LEWIS: ...he did. We know he did.

JAN: I didn't finish. Imagine he sent them as a test. A challenge. A trial.

CAROLINE: Do you remember Dick's story his friend, the spy? I mean a real spy. He was being interrogated and he just sat there and defied them and pulled out his *own* fingernails.

LEWIS: Dick said they were his own pliers, but it was all just a joke.

JAN: Was it?

LEWIS: Of course it was a joke.

JAN: I'm not certain.

LEWIS: Oh, you suit yourself.

CAROLINE: What are you playing at now Jan?

JAN: Go on Lewis, be brave.

LEWIS: Don't start that again! I'll ask you to leave.

JAN: I'm going soon.

LEWIS: Good.

JAN: But I'd like to see you be brave first.

CAROLINE: Let it drop now Jan. It's not funny.

LEWIS: Go on then. Tell me what you want me to do.

JAN: Take the pliers and pull out a fingernail.

LEWIS: You mean one of yours?

JAN: No, one of your own.

LEWIS: I'm not stupid.

JAN: One of mine then.

CAROLINE: Pack it in now. I'm going back to work.

LEWIS: You're on.

(*LEWIS picks up the pliers. Jan extends his hand.*)

JAN: There. Which nail? Choose one.

LEWIS: You don't mean that.

JAN: Pick one.

LEWIS: You're ridiculous.

JAN: It makes no difference to me. It'll be excruciating whichever you wrench off.

CAROLINE: Just stop it.

JAN: He's not up to it.

LEWIS: You'll see.

JAN: You'll never do it.

LEWIS: Keep watching.

JAN: I'm all eyes.

(*LEWIS positions the pliers on one of JAN's fingernails and starts to pull. Suddenly he yanks hard and JAN screams in pain, clutching his finger. LEWIS is horrified and flings the pliers across the table.*)

JAN: Ahhhhhh!

CAROLINE: What have you done Lewis?!

JAN: You maniac!

LEWIS: I was invited.

CAROLINE: Let me look.

LEWIS: Do we need an ambulance?

JAN: Don't touch it!

LEWIS: A tourniquet?

JAN: You twat!

LEWIS: You goaded me.

CAROLINE: Let me look.

(CAROLINE grasps JAN's hand and examines the finger.)

CAROLINE: It's only the tip. We won't need an ambulance. You can stop squawking now Jan. *(CAROLINE points at LEWIS)* You're bonkers *(CAROLINE points at JAN)* and you're just as bad.

JAN: It's agony.

LEWIS: I can't see any blood.

(CAROLINE picks up the pliers and puts them back in the box.)

CAROLINE: *(quietly)* Dick sent us those. You shouldn't let yourself be provoked so quickly.

LEWIS: Who?

CAROLINE: Both of you.

LEWIS: Satisfied Jan?

(*JAN shrugs.*)

CAROLINE: Shall we pack it all away?

LEWIS: What is Dick playing at?

JAN: It was an excuse to push us all together.

LEWIS: God forbid.

CAROLINE: We see each other all the time.

LEWIS: Perhaps we shouldn't then.

JAN: Have you only just got there?

LEWIS: I thought we were all friends.

JAN: We were until you tried to rip my finger off.

CAROLINE: No, you're wrong. We weren't friends, not really. We were all friends with Dick but you two can't stand each other and you both think I'm stupid.

(*LEWIS and CAROLINE freeze.*)

JAN: (*to audience*) So this is my big chance. All I have to do is to tell Caroline that I've always thought she was highly intelligent and tell Lewis there's no hard feelings and we're good buddies. Then tonight we'll all meet up, like we always do.

(*LEWIS and CAROLINE unfreeze.*)

LEWIS: So you think we're flogging a dead horse? Both of you?

JAN: Dead.

LEWIS: What?

JAN: The horse is decomposed. We've been down to the scraps in the last few months.

CAROLINE: So, neither of you are going to deny that you think I'm stupid.

(Neither JAN or LEWIS move or say anything but sit glaring across the table at each other.)

CAROLINE: *(Quietly and steadily)* Right. Right. Ignore the thick hairdresser. I've got customers waiting. And I do read poetry, you know. Extensively.

(CAROLINE exits.)

JAN: Poetry?
I wish I were a caterpillar
My life would be a farce
I'd climb up to the top of trees...

LEWIS: ...Jan, you also know where the door is...

JAN: ... and slide down on my hands and knees.

(JAN rises to leave.)

JAN: Dick made up the story about the pliers. He had a good sense of the absurd.

(JAN takes a small box of paracetamol from his pocket and puts them on the table.)

LEWIS: What's that?

JAN: Supermarket brand paracetamol. They're yours and I'm giving them back. I got them out of your jacket pocket in the hallway on my way in.

LEWIS: Have you got a headache?

JAN: No.

LEWIS: I don't understand you.

JAN: Obviously.

LEWIS: This was all a waste of an afternoon. Make sure you the door shut properly when you go.

(*Exit JAN. LEWIS turns on the radio. Music is playing. He repacks the items in the box and exits to another room in his flat. The music fades out and there is a news bulletin.*)

RADIO: *(V/O:)* This is the CCB news at four o'clock. Directors of the Tate Gallery have just confirmed the partial theft of the Turner Prize winning artwork, "Car boot in the Sideboard" by eminent artist, Lucy Killamarsh. The exhibits disappeared during public opening hours at the gallery yesterday afternoon. Police are currently interviewing Gallery staff and checking CCTV footage. There are unconfirmed reports that the items are being held to ransom by a little known human rights group. Items stolen from the artwork include a shuttlecock, a pair of pliers, a bar of soap and a small wooden clog. Miss Killamarsh is said to be inconsolable. *(Pause:)* The government are due to release new figures on unemployment later today following the closure of a pair of particularly threadbare orange curtains left over from...

(*Radio fades. Lights fade.*)

The End

A Downmarket Tragedy

Professor Sophie Watson placed particular stress on the ability of markets to act as a social focus for the local community, providing a space where different groups of people (across age, race and ethnicity) can mix casually with one another, thus breaking down potential hostilities between different groups, and acting as a space of social inclusion.

- From *'Can the traditional market survive?'* – Communities and Local Government Committee at www.parliament.uk

Synopsis

Danny Palmer, a 40-year-old market trader is finding things tough and supplements his income through doing a Roy Orbison tribute act. When the play opens mother Jacky is minding the market stall while Danny goes to the dentist. She is concerned about Danny, how hard he is working and the general state of trade on the market. She talks to Ralph, the "veg man" who is about to retire. They reflect upon how things have changed for the markets.

When Danny returns, he is not in a good way. Jacky goes to do a little shopping and to buy a retirement card for Ralph from the stall run by old friend Vera. She is shocked when Danny tells her that Vera no longer trades and has been declared bankrupt. While Jacky is away, Danny summons Zena, another market trader. He divulges that the bank is calling in his overdraft and he wants Zena to return some money she borrowed from him a while ago. When he reveals the money is to purchase stock from sources Zena considers non-ethical, she refuses to pay him back. They argue, culminating in Zena slapping Danny. Jacky sees this and is suspicious but Danny won't tell her of his financial difficulties.

Jacky has bought a lottery scratch-card for Ralph as she cannot buy a retirement card and goes to give it to him. Danny leaves his pitch for a few minutes and a young lad mindlessly vandalises his stall, which only increases Danny's desperation. In the meanwhile, Ralph is overjoyed that he has won £100,000 on the scratch card gifted to him by Jacky and Danny is secretly devastated. Then Zena returns telling them to phone an ambulance as they have found Vera's grandson – the same boy who vandalised Danny's stall – collapsed at the back of the market toilet block, probably the result of taking a form of impure MDMA or similar. Before the ambulance arrives we hear that the boy is already dead. This is almost too much for Danny, truly a day of "straws and camels' backs" and he wants to pack up his business. Jacky realises that the press attention resulting from the death might be good for business and convinces Danny he must keep going.

Cast

Jacky Palmer – *Early 60's. Retired and widowed.*

Danny Palmer – *Jacky's son. Runs a shirt and t. shirt stall on a small market. Does a Roy Orbison Tribute Act in the evenings. Aged 40.*

Ralph Reardon – *72 yrs old. Longstanding "veg man" on the market. Red faced, still fit and active.*

Zena – *Mid-thirties. Owns the flower stall on the market. Her style is very much "hippy chic".*

Ryan – *In teens. Pale and thin. Wears a black sweatshirt with the hood pulled up. Hearing impaired and unable to speak. (May be doubled with the actor who plays Zena or Ralph, as necessary.)*

Setting

A typical open air market in a provincial town. It is mid-morning in early December and the weather is more than usually raw, overcast and grim. Various market stalls may be visible, but it is only necessary to show Danny's shirt stall. This includes a long table with various carefully folded piles of shirts. At the rear of the stall is a high rail where shirts and the prices etc. are displayed on coat hangers.

JACKY PALMER stands beside the stall. She wears a padded jacket, trousers, gloves and a woolly hat, but is still freezing cold. The market is very near deserted. RYAN stands before the stall but not close to JACKY. He stares out to the audience without focus. JACKY glances pointedly across at him a couple of times and eventually we see she decides to speak.

JACKY: You are all right, aren't you? *(Waits for answer)* It's a cold day just to be standing around. Are you looking for something? *(Pause)* Are you waiting for a mate?

RYAN looks at her and then turns and leaves. JACKY sighs heavily. Enter RALPH REARDON. He embraces JACKY playfully from behind and she turns in surprise. JACKY'S mood brightens immediately.

JACKY: Ralph Reardon!

RALPH: Hello Jacky my love.

JACKY: I don't think I've ever seen you when you're not standing behind that stall. See, you've got legs!

RALPH: Yea, that's what everyone's saying and I tell you what, I'm just about to use 'em.

JACKY: What do you mean? What's happening Ralph? Are you running a marathon?

RALPH: I've just been out from behind the stall most of the morning, saying goodbye to folk, before I walk away.

JACKY: Saying goodbye?

RALPH: Didn't Danny tell you? I'm packing it in. Retiring.

JACKY: You're never sixty-five Ralph!

RALPH: Sixty-five? I've gone seventy-two this year.

JACKY: You don't look it. What a shame though; you're a legend on this market.

RALPH: What's left of this market!

JACKY: But why finish now?

RALPH: They're putting the rent up again.

JACKY: Danny never said.

RALPH: Well perhaps it don't affect him as much. I need a double pitch for my veg and it hits you harder.

JACKY: Of course it does.

RALPH: Then there's the cost of diesel. I have to go out and fetch new stock for every market. It's not like locking a couple of sacks of tee shirts in your garden shed.

JACKY: Danny pays for a lock up.

RALPH: But you know what I mean. Anyway, I'm out of it.

JACKY: I am sorry Ralph. It won't be the same without you here. Is one of your kids taking over?

RALPH: Oh no. Our Julie works for an insurance company now and she wouldn't be caught dead on a veg stall and our Mickey's set up his own business as a mechanic.

JACKY: Can you sell it?

RALPH: What's there to sell? The stock's perishable and the van's knackered. And as to my good name, who cares about that?

JACKY: But there'll be no one doing fresh veg when you're gone.

RALPH: Someone will move in. The Lewis clan from Bemrose Market – they might be interested – but p'haps not. These superstore supermarkets sell same as us and they can get things all year round that we don't get near. If they hadn't stuck that bugger right there on the other side of the road, then it might not be so bad.

JACKY: Sad business. Look, I wish my Danny was back. He'd like to see you. I know he would.

RALPH: Where's he gone? I didn't think you did the stall any more.

JACKY: I don't usually – just stand in now and then, when Danny needs to get away. He's at the dentist this morning, then calling in at the bank or som'ert.

RALPH: Doesn't his wife step in?

JACKY: What? Gina? Just like your Julie; wouldn't be caught dead shopping here, let alone working here. I've told her all about fresh air and wholesomeness but there's always some excuse about having to be at home for the nippers. But they ain't nippers now; the youngest's gone fourteen.

(Enter DANNY. His look of concern goes beyond the tooth he has just had pulled and the bloodied handkerchief he holds to his mouth. He carries a sports bag and a guitar case which he tosses underneath the stall.)

JACKY: Oh, here he is. Speak of the devil and he puts in an appearance...(*She notices DANNY's mouth*)...Danny, what happened?

DANNY: Nothing Mum. He had to pull a tooth and you know I bleed like a hysterical hog.

JACKY: As long as that's all it is.

DANNY: It is. Anyway, Ralph what are you doing here? See Mum, he does have legs despite the malicious rumours.

JACKY: We've done that joke Danny. Ralph's just come to see us. He's finishing today.

DANNY: Oh yea, of course. (*He shakes RALPH'S hand*) Well good luck mate. You'll be missed.

RALPH: Thanks Danny. Nice to catch you, but I want to get round and see everyone – so I'm finished early this afternoon.

DANNY: Well, come back and visit us.

RALPH: I will.

(*JACKY kisses RALPH on the cheek.*)

JACKY: He means it. Come back and see us.

RALPH: You take care of yourself.

JACKY: Bye Ralph.

RALPH: Bye Jacky.

(*Exit RALPH.*)

DANNY: How's business been Mum?

JACKY: Dead as an Alma Cogan revival concert on a Tuesday night. Not sold a thing all morning.

DANNY: It's that time of year.

JACKY: It's December Danny! Things should be geeing up for Christmas. I never knew it this quiet in my days here.

DANNY: It'll pick up. It's better on Saturdays.

JACKY: No wonder Ralph's retiring. I do wish you'd have told me about that. I would've got him a nice card.

DANNY: Ralph won't mind. Anyway, you kissed him. He'll live off that for the next three months.

JACKY: He used to fancy me; that was before we both started to look like we'd been made from crepe paper. Your Dad threatened to thump him once or twice. But look at you. Did the dentist really have to snatch your tooth out? Were you in pain?

DANNY: A bit. It don't hurt now.

JACKY: All that blood.

DANNY: I've got plenty.

JACKY: But couldn't he save it? Surely, crowns and root canals and the rest of the paraphernalia? There must have been something they could do without wrenching it out. It's right near the front. You'll have a gap when you smile.

DANNY: Well there's been no call for that lately.

JACKY: Danny! What is the matter?

DANNY: Everything's fine Mum. Yea, they could have put a crown on it, but it costs a fortune and takes hours; I just wasn't in the mood today. I went for the quick fix option Mum.

JACKY: So if you broke your leg would you tell 'em to hack it off and not to plaster it 'cause you wasn't in the mood? Danny? Would you? *(DANNY'S mobile begins to ring.)* There you are, saved by the bell.

(DANNY gets his mobile out of his pocket and starts to talk into it).

DANNY: Hi, Gina....ok?....no I haven't got round to it yet. ...yea...yea...by this afternoon....I promise.....see you later Babe.

(The 'phone call terminates.)

JACKY: Gina?

DANNY: Yea.

JACKY: You know, I do wish I'd got Ralph a card or something.

DANNY: There's plenty in the supermarket over there.

JACKY: Supermarket! There's no need to go there. I'll just pop over to Vera Clutterbuck's stall.

DANNY: She's not there anymore.

JACKY: What? Vera doesn't do the cards anymore? You'll be telling me next that grass has taken to growing purple instead of green.

DANNY: She's been gone nearly a year. Bankrupt.

JACKY: I don't believe it. Vera Clutterbuck bankrupt! *(She sighs)* It's been a telling morning. Hardly any punters around. You're all right though, aren't you Danny? You would tell me if you weren't getting by?

DANNY: We're fine Mum.

JACKY: Everything was okay at the bank wasn't it? You were gone such a long time.

DANNY: Yea Mum. It was the tooth that took ages and on top of that, I've got a gig tonight and I had to sort it – you know, get my gear so I can go straight there when I've finished here.

JACKY: I suppose that's good but I don't like the idea of you having to do another job on top of doing the market.

DANNY: The gig's money for old rope. It pays really well and it's a laugh.

JACKY: Long as it keeps you laughing. Even with a gap in your teeth. *(Fumbling in her pocket, she pulls out a lottery scratch card.)* Hey, look what's in here. Lottery scratch card.

DANNY: Is it a winner?

JACKY: I dunno. I haven't scratched it yet. I got it yesterday when I went to fetch the papers and then I forgot all about it.

DANNY: You're probably walking 'round with a million quid in your pocket. Do you want tuppence?

JACKY: No, I'm not scratching it myself. I'm giving it to Ralph.

DANNY: You're daft Mum.

JACKY: Maybe, but I've got no other card and if it's a winner, he can get himself a nice bottle of Jack Daniels or something. If it ain't, then it's the thought that counts.

DANNY: He went that way.

JACKY: I'll catch him up then.

(As JACKY leaves, DANNY starts poking around in his sports bag. Enter ZENA.)

DANNY: Zena! Just the person.

ZENA: Has the old groper gone?

DANNY: Ralph?

ZENA: Yea, he's using this retirement malarkey to do the circuit, snogging every woman on the market.

DANNY: Mum's just gone after him.

ZENA: I hope you sent a chaperone.

DANNY: She can handle herself.

ZENA: He squeezed my bum.

DANNY: If he does that to Mum, she'll slug him. Anyway, I need to talk to you while the place is empty.

ZENA: You expecting a coach load to turn up?

DANNY: I've been to the bank.

ZENA: Nice for you.

DANNY: It wasn't.

ZENA: Really?

DANNY: I went for a loan. They said "no". Straight out, "no" and then they said they're calling in the overdraft.

ZENA: With no notice? They can't do that, surely?

DANNY: They can. Ever read the small print of an overdraft agreement? That's exactly what they can do. Oh yea, they've given me a month to get it sorted. Sorted by the fifth of January or else.

ZENA: That's shit. Twelfth night as well.

DANNY: Shush Zena. Mum's coming. I don't want her to know.

(JACKY returns)

ZENA : Hi Jacky.

JACKY: Hello Zena love. How are you doing?

ZENA: Fine thanks.

JACKY: How's business?

ZENA: Not too bad. I've been doing outside the bone yard on Sunday mornings – just from the back of the van, but it's quite lucrative.

JACKY: That's good then.

DANNY: Are you off now Mum?

JACKY: I thought I might do a bit of my own shopping while I'm here. Do you want me to bring you back a cup of tea?

DANNY: Please.

JACKY: Do you want one Zena?

ZENA: No thanks. I'll have to get back to my pitch in a minute.

DANNY: Rush, is there?

ZENA: *(Ignoring DANNY'S comment)* Kath's watching it.

JACKY: What about Vera Clutterbuck then?

ZENA: Yea. Shame. She'd been here a long time.

DANNY: Tragic.

JACKY: It's criminal! Who knows where it will end.

DANNY: Don't let it wind you up Mum.

JACKY: Hard not to but I'd better get on with me shopping.

(Exit JACKY.)

ZENA: Your Mum's right. Where will it end? Half the stalls are empty and about one punter to every six stalls that are open. They'll end up shutting this place.

DANNY: And you came over here to lighten my life?

ZENA: Sorry Danny, but someone should be doing something. Did you know that this place was set up by Royal Charter in 1207?

DANNY: You'd think Royalty would have something better to do.

ZENA: Don't take the rip Danny. There's been a market here for eight hundred years. They stick preservation orders on buildings and you can't do a thing to them without special permission. Yet, they can run this place into the ground after eight hundred years and nobody gives a sod. It doesn't happen in France or Turkey...

DANNY: ...your favourite holiday destinations...

ZENA: Anywhere but England!

DANNY: Ralph said it was the way things were going.

ZENA: Of course, the United Nations consult Ralph Reardon when they're stuck for the solution to Third World poverty! And I suppose he had you feeling sorry for him. Well, I wouldn't, if I were you. Did you know that he's got three properties in Spain?

DANNY: You're joking!

ZENA: Ralph can give you a right lecture about the big faceless organisations against the little man. You've heard him. No more individuals. The little man get squeezed out and there are supermarkets everywhere who can put sprouts on your dinner plate in high summer and strawberries with your turkey on Christmas day. The future and the past totally frozen for your convenience and then the microwave pings and it all comes to life again. Cheap, crap food, but then again it comes nicely packaged so, who cares? The butcher, the baker, the candlestick maker and the market trader are all buggered because they can't compete. He says it and it's all bloody true of course, but what does it matter to an old sod like Ralph with so much to fall back on. A case of the wrong prats saying the right things – he's a born politician.

DANNY: *(Sadly)* I'm being squeezed out Zena. The supermarkets, the chain stores, the internet – well, they might just as easily slit my guts and watch the blood flow into the gutter. Then they suck it up and make black pudding.

ZENA: Danny, please!

DANNY: I've always tried to sell local stuff but I just can't make a profit anymore.

ZENA: Are things that bad for you?

DANNY: Worse. Mum's concerned that we haven't had a sale all morning – well, not even a sale, an interested punter would be start. If I do sell, the profit's so small you'd need a microscope to see it.

ZENA: Bloody hell, Danny.

DANNY: All that's left is to offer up are some really cheap imports.

ZENA: So, what's out there?

DANNY: You know, the usual stuff from the Far East. If I can get a load and punt it on quickly with the prices chopped, I might see it through to the other side of Christmas.

ZENA: But that'll be real sweatshop stuff run up by little kiddies.

DANNY: Kid's whose alternative is to flog their ass.

ZENA: That's a glib "get out" clause Danny. You always said you were only interested in quality.

DANNY: Quality isn't working at the moment, not on this market stall. Let's face it Zena, who wants to prowl about a miserable hole like this with a sky that looks fit to slash its own wrists, when you can go "click, click" on the internet and they'll stick it in the post to you? You know what, I think the days of the market are long over but we were so busy being "authentic" that we didn't catch on 'till now.

ZENA: You defeatist bastard. You just have to keep going...

DANNY: ...like the hundred years war?...

ZENA: ...If people like you give up, then big business will win. Listen, the punters are out there; they've just forgotten that we're here.

DANNY: (*DANNY laughs loudly and almost falsely:*) Just listen to Mother Courage dragging her flower cart behind her.

ZENA: I don't know what you're talking about, but you go along the cheap import route and you're sunk – in every sense, sunk.

DANNY: Zena, I wasn't asking either your opinion or your permission about my potential choice of supplier.

ZENA: Is this your new side line? Pomposity? What did you want me for? You said you wanted to see me.

DANNY: Yea, I did.

ZENA: Well, then?

DANNY: The money I lent you Zena. I need it back.

ZENA: Oh.

DANNY: For God's sake, you've got it by now.

ZENA: Not really. It isn't that easy.

DANNY: It's been two years Zena!

ZENA: But Danny, when you lent me the money you said I could take as long as I liked to pay it back.

DANNY: As long as you "needed" not "liked".

ZENA: Well, no time limit was set.

DANNY: I was thinking months, not years.

ZENA: I can probably scrape some of it together.

DANNY: That would be a start. Look, I'm not meaning to put you under pressure here, but my back's against the wall and there's a bulldozer revving up on the other side of it.

ZENA: Like you say, no pressure intended.

DANNY: Please Zena.

ZENA: I'll do what's possible. Just give me until after the weekend to get a few things sorted....and I don't suppose it's the right time to ask a favour?

DANNY: Does it involve money?

ZENA: No.

DANNY: Fire away then.

ZENA: Well, it's about that Roy Orbison tribute act you do.

DANNY: Oh yea.

ZENA: Well, I got involved in an animal rights charity evening and I promised I'd turn something up in the way of entertainment – well, I did nothing about it and it's just two weeks away and I'm going to look like a right Charlie, aren't I? It's like, "What's the show tonight Zena?" – "Well nothing actually – I forgot. Shall we have a game of tiddly-winks?" You know where this is leading?

DANNY: Are you asking me to be the entertainment for nothing? For free?

ZENA: Yes, Danny, yes.

DANNY: Then the answer's no, Zena, no. I only do Roy when there's a payment involved.

ZENA: But I can't pay you. It's for charity.

DANNY: Then I can't do it.

ZENA: Just an hour – and I'll pay your expenses myself.

DANNY: How? You're meant to be struggling to pay back a loan – a loan you wheedled out of a vulnerable mate several eons ago. No Zena. The answer's no.

ZENA: But why? You're usually so helpful.

DANNY: Just how much pleasure do you think it gives me to prance about in a black bling-encrusted shirt bellowing out "Crying"?

ZENA: Why do you do it then?

DANNY: Because I bloody well have to. It's the only thing that's paying at the moment – it puts bread and Kentucky Fried Chicken on the table....

ZENA: ...and lashings of Pandora around Gina's wrists!

DANNY: Leave her out of it. And yea, I'll do as many gigs as I can while they still pay but I'm not pummelling salt in the ulcer by doing it for free.

ZENA: I thought you enjoyed it.

DANNY: ...when it was just fun – now it's become necessary.

ZENA: Look, I'm sure you'll feel better about it when you've got the bank off your back. I'll try to get everything I owe you as quickly as I can then you can see the bank manager. But do us favour and give a thought to this animal rights do.

DANNY: The money won't be going to the bank manager – it's to invest in this new stock.

ZENA: If that's what you're intending, then I won't be able to find the money so quickly.

DANNY: It's not yours to hang on to.

ZENA: But there's a question of morality involved.

DANNY: You should be out of breath – the speed with which you run up to the moral high ground and then hog it like you'd bought the freehold.

ZENA: Somebody's got to!

DANNY: And who gave you the patent rights on morality?

ZENA: For God's sake Danny!

DANNY: So that's who it was. God! Just look at you Zena. Sitting like a vulture at the cemetery gates offering chrysanths at inflated prices. Half the poor sods there are usually too upset to remember to bring their own and they just can't walk past the emotional blackmail in your face, as you stand strategically placed to thrust your cheap lilies at unreasonable prices into their tears. I know your game Zena. You go on about Ralph, but you're worse. At least he pushes a joke with his spuds.

(Re-enter JACKY, just as ZENA slaps DANNY hard across the face in anger.)

ZENA: Bastard!

JACKY: What's going on?

ZENA: Sorry Jacky.

(ZENA stalks off.)

JACKY: Well, what's going on?

DANNY: A misunderstanding.

JACKY: It must have been more than that to make her take a swipe at you.

DANNY: It was nothing. She just gets wound up.

JACKY: Is there something between you and Zena?

DANNY: Of course not!

JACKY: I hope you're right 'cause you know what Gina's like. She'll take the kids, the house, everything.

DANNY: It's nothing like that Mum

JACKY: Didn't look like it.

DANNY: Just leave it!

JACKY: You want to fall out with me as well? I'll give you as good a clout round the head as Zena can, just mark my words.

DANNY: What's the matter with you all today?

JACKY: It must be weather. Sorry. I'm getting too old to stand out in this cold.

DANNY: Go home Mum. Go and get warm.

JACKY: I'm not finished yet. Look I'll just do this shopping then I'll come back and see you before you go home. I've still got to get your tea.

(JACKY departs. DANNY stands for a few moments before RYAN enters. RYAN looks intently through some of the stock on DANNY'S store and then seems to openly sneer.)

DANNY: Did you want something? Lost the power of speech, have you?

(RYAN makes the "wanker" sign with his right hand.)

DANNY: Oh, just piss off yourself. Go on. *(Bitterly)* I'm only interested if you're giving me money. They'll put that on my gravestone.

(RYAN exits. DANNY walks up and down for a moment or two looking uncomfortable. He goes behind the stall and ferrets out a cardboard sign and props it up against the stall. The sign says "call of nature – back in 5 minutes". DANNY exits. Within moments, RYAN returns. He drags some of the stock from the stall onto the floor, generally making a mess of it and throwing it around. Then he spots DANNY's sports bag under the stall. He snatches it out and disgorges the contents. He pulls out DANNY's "Roy Orbison" shirt and holds it up. Very carefully he lays it flat on the floor. He fumbles around in his pocket and pulls out a can of spray paint. At the same time a small plastic wrapped packet falls from his pocket and lands on the ground. He looks around for the first time and then puts the packet carefully back in his pocket. Using the paint can, he sprays something across the back of the shirt. He looks at his work for a moment and then screws it into a ball and throws it behind the stall. RYAN exits and DANNY returns within moments)

DANNY: What the...? Jesus Christ...! Shit!!!

(ZENA enters hurriedly.)

ZENA: What happened Danny?

DANNY: You tell me. I wasn't here?

ZENA: I saw nothing.

DANNY: You sure?

ZENA: Oh, stuff you! I was concerned! Some bastard's wrecked your stall.

DANNY: And did you stand watching Zena? Cheering them on from the sidelines?

(Re-enter JACKY with a plastic carrier and a Styrofoam cup of tea.)

ZENA: You wanker! Don't be so pathetic.

JACKY: Don't start again! What's been goin' on here?

DANNY: I left the stall for two minutes and this is what I come back to.

JACKY: Why didn't you tell someone to watch it for you. I'm sure Zena would have…

DANNY: …I'm sure she did; every moment, while some bastard did this. Bit of free entertainment for you Love?

JACKY: You don't really think that anyone on this market would just stand there and watch some vandal do this to one of us?

ZENA: That's right Danny!

DANNY: God save me from the precious market brotherhood – or should it be sisterhood these days - where we all stick together and no one outdoes anyone else. Did you know Mum, that after they declared Vera bankrupt, the poor old sod kept working her stall even though they were meant to shut her down. She just kept turning up and then they sent the bailiffs in and they took Vera's van and chucked all of her birthday cards, the wrapping paper and those ribbon bow things into a soggy cardboard box, all churned up and squashed in the mud. That was Vera' stock – her life – and they carted it off with everyone looking and all the time our gritty Boudica *(indicating ZENA)* was true to form and just stood there, along with some of the other witches on this market. They just let them storm the ramparts. They just let them do it.

ZENA: What could we do? They had all the paperwork.

DANNY: Paperwork! Pathetic!

JACKY: This isn't getting this mess sorted Danny. Come on. We'll all pitch in. I'm sure Zena will help.

DANNY: She's got her own stall to watch. Better get back there quick; might be a serial market vandal on the loose. He'll be having the tops off your daffs.

ZENA: Wrong time of year for daffs. Come on I'll give you a hand. I can see my pitch from here and it's not busy at the moment.

DANNY: Just like you can see mine.

ZENA: *(Angrily)* Believe me Danny, I saw nothing!

JACKY: Pack it in you two!

(JACKY and ZENA start to pick the shirts up and carefully place them back on the stall. After a few moments DANNY joins in.)

ZENA: Any idea who might have done this?

DANNY: There was a lad hanging around earlier, just before I went to the loo. I had to tell him to sod off.

ZENA: What was he doing?

DANNY: Nothing really. He just annoyed me.

(ZENA and JACKY exchange meaningful looks as though to say "well that wouldn't be hard".)

DANNY: He looked like all the kids look. About fifteen. Black hoodie. In good need of a wash and a scrub with Clearasil.

JACKY: He was hanging around earlier.

ZENA: Black hoodie? Did he talk to you?

JACKY: He seemed to have nothing to say.

ZENA: He wouldn't. It was Vera Clutterbuck's grandson – Ryan. He's hearing-impaired and he doesn't speak.

JACKY: I remember. I thought he was only three or four.

ZENA: He might have been when you last saw him.

JACKY: Poor little sod.

(JACKY picks up the Roy Orbison shirt from the back of the stall, which is still in a screwed-up ball)

JACKY: What's this Danny?

(She passes it to him and he unrolls it.)

DANNY: My Roy Orbison kit. *(He holds it against himself. The word "wanker" is clearly displayed.)* Oh no! I'll never get this out.

JACKY: That's a bit mean, even if he is disabled.

ZENA: Perhaps it's the only way he can express himself.

DANNY: And what do you think he was trying to say?

ZENA: It was probably frustration.

DANNY: Perhaps I should wear it like this tonight. It'd show what the world thinks of me. Perhaps what I think of myself. Come on Zena. Look. There's someone at you stall. You'd better go back.

ZENA: Yea. I'm sorry Danny.

(Exit ZENA.)

JACKY: At least someone's doing business. Shows it isn't hopeless. Probably be an uphill slog getting things back to what they were - all guts and hard work. You know that Danny. No quick fix, no easy way to mend it. I know that's what you're hoping for. I can't blame you though, when it's all left to you to do everything. Gina doesn't exactly pull her weight, does she? I blame myself as well though; giving you the easy way out as a nipper. You know, when you was about two years old I used to keep a box of biscuits on the stairs and I'd give you one when we was going out the front door. It was a bribe really, a way of making you co-operate. You know what little kids are when you're trying to get them through the front door in a hurry - clamping their arms by their sides so you can't get their coats on and losing a glove. You must know. You've got kids yourself. Awkward as hell. I wonder what makes us love the little buggers so much? Anyway, most mornings you used to break the biscuit and then you'd start crying and howling, "Mend it! Mend it!". So, I'd get the broken biscuit and put it back in the biscuit tin, say a magic spell and then I'd fetch it out whole again. Of course, it wasn't mended; it was just another biscuit but you wouldn't know that and I'd never break the magic and tell you. Perhaps I should have just said "It's broken and it can't be fixed" or even "eat it in two halves; it tastes just the same". I wonder what's harder; telling a forty-year-old the truth or a two-year-old?

(Enter RALPH, ecstatically happy.)

RALPH: Jacky!

JACKY: Back again Ralph? Or are you going now?

RALPH: Jacky, you little gem!

JACKY: Have you been having a drink Ralph? Sun's not over the yard arm yet – need to watch your liver when you get to our age.

RALPH: You pudding! I'm not drunk – well I am really. Drunk with joy.

JACKY: I didn't think you wanted to retire that much!

RALPH: Jacky, it's that scratch card you gave me. Here, give us a hug.

JACKY: I see. You've won something Ralph?

RALPH: Just look here. *(He thrusts the scratch card into her hand. JACKY gasps).* See, it's the big one. Hundred thousand pounds.

DANNY: A hundred thousand pounds?

RALPH: That's right. A hundred thousand. And your lovely mother gave it to me.

(RALPH kisses JACKY loudly on the cheek.)

JACKY: I'm so pleased for you Ralph!

DANNY: *(Rye, but choked)* That's heck of a "Good Luck on Your Retirement" card Mum.

JACKY: It's brilliant. Who'd have guessed?

RALPH: I'll get you something nice.

JACKY: You don't have to do that Ralph.

RALPH: Oh, come on. I remember you used to like posh scent, didn't you? You get up town and get yourself a bottle. I'll pay for it - just save me the receipt.

JACKY: That's kind Ralph.

RALPH: And get Danny a nice bottle of Jack Daniels. I've seen it on offer at the supermarket over there at the moment. That's what you like to drink, isn't it son?

DANNY: *(Ungraciously)* Yea, Jack Daniels. I can drink to your good luck.

JACKY: Have you told your wife yet Ralph?

RALPH: I'm just going to 'phone her now.

JACKY: Danny, lend Ralph your mobile.

DANNY: Yea, why not?

RALPH: It's all right. I'll use the pay 'phone in the supermarket. I don't like mobiles – I'm old fashioned like that. *(He gives JACKY another big hug.)* Well thanks again Sweetheart. You really know how to give a bloke a send-off.

(Exit RALPH.)

DANNY: *(Bitterly)* Nice one Mum. You really know how to make a poor old bloke very happy....

(Enter ZENA urgently.)

ZENA: ...Danny give us your mobile.

DANNY: Another one! I'm not a public facility. Haven't you got your own?

ZENA: Shut up Danny! Battery's dead. We need to call an ambulance.

JACKY: It's not Ralph, is it?

ZENA: No, it's Ryan - Vera Clutterbuck's grandson. I found him collapsed.

(DANNY talks into his mobile)

DANNY: Ambulance please – yea...yea....urgent...someone's collapsed...I don't know...

ZENA: I'd better get back to him – back of the toilet block Danny.

JACKY: I'll come with you.

DANNY: Portsfold Market – yea...you need to go to the Silver Street entrance...there's a toilet block – back of the toilet block...that's right....I dunno. The person who found him asked me to call....male, yes...a youth....they've gone back to him so I don't know..... Okay...I'll tell 'em. Oh, you can tell 'em yourself... they're here.... (*Enter ZENA. DANNY tries to give her the mobile but she waves him off. He speaks into the mobile again.)....* My mistake. Look how long before the ambulance gets here.... Yea, yea....thank you. *(He puts the mobile back in his pocket)* They reckon no more than ten minutes on the ambulance. They said to put a blanket over him and keep him warm but not to move him.

ZENA: No point Danny. He's already gone.

DANNY: Are you sure? He's a kid.

ZENA: Yea. Your Mum said and ...and she seems to know. Greg from "Tyres–R–Us" is there as well. He's doing CPR but nothing's happening, nothing's changing. Greg says he did a first aid course but it doesn't seem to be much use.

DANNY: But how? What happened? My lad's his age.

ZENA: Here this. *(She fetches a little plastic packet – the same packet that Ryan had earlier but now clearly ripped open – out of her pocket)* There was this little packet... some sort of drug I suppose.

DANNY: Stupid little sod.

ZENA: Dead little sod.

(Enter JACKY, almost tearful. DANNY gives her a hug.)

JACKY: What a day!

ZENA: What's happening?

JACKY: Greg's still trying but... *(she shrugs hopelessly)*. He said he'd stay with him. I think you'll have to talk to the police Zena. You were first there.

ZENA: Okay. I'll get some flowers off my stall. We'll leave them there after they've moved him.

(Exit ZENA.)

DANNY: I suppose we'd better pack up.

JACKY: No Danny. It's not time to pack up. Now's the time to keep going.

DANNY: ....but with what's happened...

JACKY: ....yea, the name of the market in the papers – maybe even on the news, then people will remember we exist.

DANNY: That's a bit callous. I know the little sod annoyed me but I wouldn't have wished for this. I'm packing up and going home. I'm finished. It's been a day of straws and camel's backs.

JACKY: Now isn't the time to chuck it in. This is an important chance for you Danny. You'll need all of your stock down from the lock up. Think about how you put it out. There'll be more punters here tomorrow than you'll have seen in a month.

DANNY: I didn't think you could be like that Mum.

JACKY: It's called survival Danny and we all play dirty sometime. Come on. Help me straighten this stall. It's still not as it should be.

(Lights fade. There is the distant sound of an ambulance siren that is fast approaching.)

The End

Printed in Dunstable, United Kingdom